"Ah-ha!" She put her hands on her hips and stared at him, her eyes growing wider.

Taken aback, Frank smiled his best smile, still entranced by her beautiful eyes. "Ah-ha?" he said cautiously.

"Ah-ha. I suppose you're just like the rest of them."

"The rest of whom?" Frank knew he should turn and leave, but the flashing eyes held him as if his feet were a part of the floor.

"And what do you plan to do about the Animal Welfare Act?" She waved a rigid finger in the direction of his chest.

Frank caught the slender hand attached to the offending finger as it passed by. He felt as if he'd touched a live wire as heat surged up his arm. Her huge eyes widened even more as they locked on his, and he knew she'd felt it, too . . .

Kate Gilbert

Kate Gilbert was born and raised in northwest Arkansas. Since finishing college, she has lived and worked in various parts of the country, but has always returned eventually to her beloved Ozarks. She and her husband, Glenn, whom she met in Atlanta fifteen years ago, now live near Fayetteville, Arkansas, where they run a successful strawberry and blueberry farm.

Kate has held a wide variety of jobs, including positions in teaching and state and local government. She says: "I have always been a voracious reader, and I got into writing three years ago quite by accident and somewhat as a lark, but quickly found myself addicted. Now I write feverishly for most of the year, except during the summer farming season and blueberry harvest."

Kate and Glenn have several pets—"an overanxious German shepherd, an overweight beagle, and an overbearing calico cat."

Other Second Chance at Love books by
Kate Gilbert

MOONSHINE AND MADNESS #391

Dear Reader:

For July, our double bill is richly filled by Kate Gilbert, who made a sparkling debut with Second Chance at Love in February, and critically acclaimed romance superstar Cait Logan, who writes exclusively for Berkley. We know you'll share our delight at the way Kate has blossomed into a first-class romantic comedienne. And Cait's celebrated talents—for powerful characterization, compelling drama, and sexual tension that sizzles off the page—are sure to satisfy once again.

Warm hearts, cold noses, and whimsical humor abound in *Cupid's Campaign* (#418) by Kate Gilbert. With the aid of her feisty, blackmailing grandmother—and her own mesmerizing jade eyes—Allie Tarkington persuades dashing attorney Frank Wade to investigate the sinister disappearance of Gran's "mostly Dachsund" Dottie.... An animal-loving heiress who marches to a different drummer, Allie entices Frank from his conventional ways as they unmask a scandalous dognapping in Reedsville, Mississippi, and fall madly, irrevocably in love! Kate Gilbert's quirky crime caper should delight *Moonlighting* viewers and fans of the Disney classic *101 Dalmations*, while the novel's tasteful love scenes and trio of colorful elderly secondary characters may be especially appealing to older readers.

Winner of the 1986 *Romantic Times* Reviewer's Choice Award for Best New Author, Cait Logan created an instant sensation with her first Second Chance at Love novel, *Lady on the Line* (#325). Cait surpassed her first book with the sensual blockbuster *Rugged Glory* (#370), and has delivered yet another steamy masterpiece with *Gambler's Lady* (#419). Macho and masterful gambler Nick Santos, a modern-day "pirate" replete with leather eyepatch and arrogant swagger, hires spirited Kim Reynolds as his casino's "lady bouncer"— then wins her as his wife in a poker game! Determined to resist her husband's swashbuckling charm, Kim finds that his four-year-old daughter, Cherry, fills an aching void in her heart. Drawn into emotional intimacy by their mutual concern for the vulnerable little girl, Nick and Kim must ultimately confront the white-hot passion that flares between them.... Here's a tale to stir your passions and characters to capture your heart, especially if you cherish vintage-romance plots.

While continuing as a Second Chance at Love author, Cait will also publish her first historical romance under our Charter imprint. We're pleased to have Cait join the Berkley roster of sensuous-romance authors such as Karen Harper, Cassie Edwards, and Elaine Barbieri, and we'll let you know when her turn-of-the-century Northwestern drama is scheduled for publication.

Berkley's July romance lineup has something for every romantic taste. If your preference runs to spellbinding historical sagas, you'll surely savor bestselling-author Mary Pershall's *Roses of Glory,* set in thirteenth-century England; *Belle Marie,* an explosive tale of forbidden love and rivalry on a Southern plantation, by Laura Ashton; and Susan Shelley's account of love between a ravishing Welsh enchantress and a conquering Norman lord in the Middle Ages, *Love's Enchantment.* Regency buffs won't want to miss award-winning Elizabeth Mansfield's latest release, *Her Heart's Captain.* And those of you who favor sweet romances will want to purchase incomparable Barbara Cartland's new Camfield novel of love, *Bewildered in Berlin.*

As always, we wish you a month of happy reading—

Sincerely,

Joan Marlow

Joan Marlow
Editor
SECOND CHANCE AT LOVE
The Berkley Publishing Group
200 Madison Avenue
New York, New York 10016

SECOND CHANCE AT LOVE

KATE GILBERT
CUPID'S CAMPAIGN

BERKLEY BOOKS, NEW YORK

CUPID'S CAMPAIGN

Copyright © 1987 by Kate Gilbert

All rights reserved. No part of this publication may be reproduced or transmitted in any form or by any means, electronic or mechanical, including photocopy, recording, or any information storage and retrieval system, without permission in writing from the publisher.

Requests for permission to make copies of any part of the work should be mailed to: Permissions, Second Chance at Love, The Berkley Publishing Group, 200 Madison Avenue, New York, NY 10016.

First edition published July 1987

"Second Chance at Love" and the butterfly emblem are trademarks belonging to Jove Publications, Inc. The name "BERKLEY" and the "B" logo are trademarks belonging to Berkley Publishing Corporation.

Second Chance at Love books are published by
The Berkley Publishing Group
200 Madison Avenue, New York, NY 10016

Printed in the United States of America

10 9 8 7 6 5 4 3 2 1

**To Mother and Dottie—
a great lady and a homeless dog
who found a special love
together**

CUPID'S CAMPAIGN

Chapter One

FRANKLIN WADE FUMBLED at the collar of his wool overcoat with a heavily gloved hand, trying to pull it higher against the cold March wind that seemed to accelerate around the corners of the shopping mall. In the process, he managed to drop his campaign cards from his other gloved hand. They skittered across the parking lot like confetti, a few coming to rest with the message FRANKLIN WADE—ELECT A PROSECUTING ATTORNEY WHO CARES facing up. Frank stood for a moment trying to decide if a retrieval effort would be worthwhile, a gust of wind catching his dark blond hair and tousling it onto his forehead.

Muttering a few choice words, he stalked into the mall, hoping he had more cards in his pocket. It was Saturday, and judging from the number of cars in the parking lot he could expect to see a lot of people. Although he hated campaigning, he knew he was a damn good lawyer and had a real flair for prosecution; he wanted to be county prosecuting attorney.

His real goal was the attorney general's office in a

few years—and there'd even been talk about the governor's office. But that would be much later. Right now, he had to get through this campaign. He had serious competition in the primary, so he had to be aggressive.

Stuffing his bulky leather gloves into a pocket, he discovered the additional cards he'd hoped for. He unbuttoned his overcoat to expose the neat, well-tailored, three-piece pinstriped suit he knew people expected of lawyers, then looked up and down the mall, trying to decide where to start his smiling and handshaking. Frank was convinced that most of the people he talked to had no idea what the prosecutor did and didn't even care until somebody ripped off their house. Then they wanted blood. Yesterday. Frank composed himself. If he could become the prosecuting attorney at age thirty-two, then it would all be worth it.

Straightening to his full six feet two inches, Frank ran his hand through his windblown shock of hair and started down the mall. Frank knew he made a good impression on people, particularly women, and always made it a point to talk to women about his campaign. Frank didn't like the fact that many people voted on the basis of looks alone, but it was a fact he couldn't afford to ignore.

And he didn't ignore the heads that turned as he passed by. He flashed a dazzling smile and a wink at two teen-age girls who rushed up to get cards, then ran away giggling and twittering. Maybe the cards would get to their parents. After shaking hands with a few people, Frank headed toward a group of people who seemed to have set up a booth of some kind in the center of the mall. His long stride took him quickly and confidently to the knot of people around the booth.

At the edge of the crowd he started offering cards

and his hand. The rich, deep voice which served him so well in the courtroom caused a number of people to turn and look at him. "Hi. I'm Franklin Wade. I'd appreciate your vote in the primary for prosecuting attorney. If you have any questions about the office or my experience, I'd be happy to discuss them with you." Most people just smiled, took the card and turned away, but he knew they would remember him.

Suddenly aware that people seemed to be more interested in something near the booth than in him, Frank peered over the crowd to see what had attracted their attention. A young woman sat, Indian-style, on a quilt, surrounded by a litter of puppies and a crowd of toddlers. Taking the children's hands, one at a time, she showed them how to pet the puppies which crawled around on the quilt. Her rich contralto voice was calm and patient as she explained how they must never pick up a puppy by its legs or skin.

Frank stood mesmerized by the sound of the magnificent voice issuing forth from what he was sure was a small woman. His campaign was temporarily forgotten at the toddlers' squeals of joy as the puppies tumbled over little legs and licked small faces. All he could see of the young woman was the back of an oversized chambray shirt and the crown of a strange hat. But the children and puppies responded to her musical voice as if she were the Pied Piper. Frank moved to his left. For some reason he didn't stop to analyze, he wanted to see her face.

As she gently put the puppies back into a makeshift cage and stood, motioning for another woman to take care of them, Frank caught just a glimpse of her face. Her skin had that clear, natural quality cosmetic companies spend millions trying to duplicate. His pulse quickened, anxious to see her eyes.

She turned back to the children. "Now, gang, what do puppies and kitties need?"

A chorus of small voices squealed, "Food, wa-wa, and a warm bankie."

The young woman leaned over, hands on her knees. "What else?"

"Huggies. Puppies want a hug!" the children screamed. With that, they scrambled up and ran in search of their mothers.

Frank was impressed by what he'd heard, more impressed by what he'd felt. He looked toward the booth to see what group was in charge. Brightly colored posters caught his attention. HAVE YOU HUGGED A PUPPY TODAY? the words below a fuzzy puppy asked. Frank decided he must be in the midst of a Humane Society group and kept handing out cards, working his way toward the blanket, the puppies, and that enchanting voice.

He looked up to find her walking toward him. She looked rather like a flower child, a long paisley skirt falling to her ankles beneath the work shirt. The peculiar hat he'd noticed turned out to be a crumpled crocheted creation which Frank thought must have come from the dumpster at the Salvation Army. "Hi. I'm Franklin Wade."

At that moment, she raised her head and Frank found himself staring into huge eyes the color of old jade. He offered his hand automatically, unable to keep from staring at her. He judged her to be in her mid-twenties. She wore no makeup, but her skin shone with the delicate softness of a child. His fingers twitched with a yearning to stroke her cheek, see if it was really as satiny as it looked. He dropped his hand, realizing she was waiting for some explanation of his name. "I'm running for prosecuting attorney." He noted several wisps of deep auburn hair trailing from the hat, framing the small, perfect face.

"Ah-ha!" She put her hands on her hips and stared at him, her eyes growing wider.

Taken aback, Frank smiled his best smile, still entranced by her beautiful eyes. "Ah-ha?" he said cautiously.

"Ah-ha. I suppose you're just like the rest of them."

"The rest of whom?" Frank knew he should turn and leave, but the flashing eyes held him as if his feet were a part of the floor. He'd been in politics long enough to know a fanatic when he saw one, and he knew he'd wandered into a nest of them, one of whom only came up to his collarbone and had lovely eyes that hinted of moss and woods and . . . things.

"And what do you plan to do about the Animal Welfare Act?" She waved a rigid finger in the direction of his chest.

Frank caught the slender hand attached to the offending finger as it passed by, afraid she would start poking him. He felt as if he'd touched a live wire as heat surged up his arm. Her huge eyes widened even more as they locked on his, and he knew she'd felt it, too. She snatched her hand away, but something still crackled in the air between them.

She jammed both hands into her skirt pockets, pulling the loose shirt aside to reveal a snug black body suit. When she spoke, her voice had dropped down into the husky range. "Well?"

Frank wasn't sure what the Animal Welfare Act was, but if it was a law, he would damn sure enforce it. "Enforce it." Frank tore his eyes away from hers, suddenly aware they had drawn a crowd. A somewhat hostile crowd from the looks of it. "Did you have anything particular in mind?" Frank could usually defuse a fanatic by logical discussion. He felt confident this would be no exception.

When he broke eye contact, she appeared to regain her senses, but she took a step backward before she waved her finger at him again. "How many cases of animal abuse have you prosecuted this year?" The hostility was gone from her voice.

"Well, I'd have to check the records." He noted her retreat and the change in her voice. It was almost as if she had started something she felt obliged to finish. He caught a scent of lemon as she peered up into his face but refused to meet his eyes. "We have a lot of important cases on the docket right now."

"Ah-ha. Just as I thought. If you'd pay more attention to animal cruelty, you'd have less human cruelty. Have you hugged your dog today?" She struggled to work up a respectable mad at him.

Frank's smile faltered. "Young lady, I don't have a dog." Suddenly he knew just how the victim of a lynch mob must feel right before the horse got slapped. "But I like dogs." How could the Pied Piper have turned into Attila the Hun before his very eyes? Then he realized she was trying to deny what had passed between them —to him and to herself.

"It's not enough to like them, you have to protect them." She turned away and scooped something out of a cardboard box. Another puppy. "We saved this poor creature from certain death. Could you give him a good home?" She gently shoved the wriggling furry object next to his chest.

Cupid's Campaign 7

The sweet smell of puppy, mingled with her lemony essence, made Frank's head reel. He'd seen a sadness in those enchanting eyes as she talked about the puppy. "Uh, I live in an apartment." Frank decided it was time for a strategic retreat from this bit of insanity he'd wandered into. "Appreciate your vote." He turned and walked rapidly down the mall, ignoring the young woman's questions about how many animals had died last year in Reed county alone. He could feel her eyes on his back and fought the urge to turn around for one more look.

Frank buttoned his coat and hurried to his car. Just what he needed—flaky animal fanatics. And yet...to hell with Saturday campaigning. What he needed now was a stiff drink and a hot shower. And to forget about those remarkable eyes—eyes that had flashed and danced and gotten greener as she'd gotten madder, then had shone with a gut-wrenching sadness when she'd spoken of abandoned puppies. Maybe not a fanatic after all...maybe a woman who cared as human beings were meant to care. Turning the sports car toward home, disgusted with his bemused state of sentimentality, he once again cursed the rigmarole of running for office and his decision to participate in it.

Allison Tarkington, better known as Allie, loaded the display materials and animals from the mall booth into the back of her '56 Ford pickup. She slammed things around, still upset by the episode with the lawyer who'd been running for something-or-other. Typical lawyer with his pinstripe suit. Allie stood stock still, her hand resting on the tailgate of the ancient truck. Except that somehow he really hadn't been typical. He'd been... well, he'd been...impressive. He'd towered over her like some Viking warrior, windblown blond hair and all. Although he'd worn an overcoat, she'd had the impression of strong, wide shoulders. She sighed. Probably just an oversized coat. Yet there didn't seem to be any way to explain away those startling eyes. She'd never seen eyes quite so blue.

Angry at her daydreaming, she loaded the last box. Her arm still tingled from the jolt he'd given her when she'd waved a finger at him. Allie had done her share of finger waving since she'd been involved in animal rights work, but the results had never been quite so... shocking. She looked at the card she'd stuffed in her pocket. A prosecutor who cares, she thought. If only there were such an animal.

Allie had discovered very few people, even fewer politicians, who really cared about the plight of animals. Almost daily Allie saw and dealt with things that sickened her, things which made her want to be a plumber or something nice and safe, but in her bed late at night, she would gird her loins for the next day, knowing if she and her volunteers didn't care, who would?

But a lawyer? Memories of another lawyer flooded back to Allie. Thanks to her own good sense—and finally saying no to her mother—she had escaped that one, but it had been a close call. After that, Allie had decided animals were a lot safer when it came to involvement. Much safer.

Slamming the door on the truck camper, she got in the cab. She loved the old truck and considered it a stroke of genius on her part. She'd discovered early on that if people knew you had money, they saw you as a do-gooder. But if you dressed the part and drove a battered pickup, people thought you were committed. Besides, the whole image made her seem younger and more starry-eyed than her twenty-six years. People thought she was about eighteen and going through a phase. Allie never ceased to be amazed by people. She thought she understood animals a whole lot better.

Animals didn't love you because of your bank account like some people did. Of course, that had not been a real problem since she'd changed her lifestyle so radically. Her mother would never recover from her youngest daughter driving around town in an old pickup truck—usually loaded down with an assortment of animals.

And speaking of animals, she had to find some homes for a few of her charges over the weekend. Her house had reached the bursting point.

Allie stood in her kitchen drinking coffee on Monday morning, watching over the feeding of two stray kittens someone had dumped on her doorstep. Pretty little black tabbies near starvation, they were finally beginning to play and act the way kittens should act. Chevis, her aging German Shepherd, also stood guard over the kittens, threatening to drown them in drool. Several older cats were studiously ignoring the new arrivals, and a host of guinea pigs and hamsters in cages peered out from amidst their cedar shavings to watch the proceedings.

"Okay, gang, that's enough." She picked up the bowls and turned her orphans over to Chevis, who immediately began washing them with enough enthusiasm to bowl them over, after which he held them down with a huge paw, bathing each in turn thoroughly. Allie smiled, amazed at the old dog who took care of all the foundlings she brought home. He loved baby creatures of all kinds.

She'd just started washing up when the phone rang.

"Oh, Allie, you've got to do something," a sobbing voice wailed.

"Gran, calm down. What happened?" Allie's whole posture became rigid. Her grandmother was not a woman who cried at the drop of a hat.

"They've kidnapped Dottie," the woman wailed.

"Who, Gran?" Dottie was her grandmother's mostly Dachshund, her pride and joy.

"I don't know who. Triola and Gladys saw them. They think it's a ring of dognappers who are working the neighborhood. You've got to do something, Allie."

Allie calmed her grandmother and assured her help was on its way, although she had serious reservations about any eyewitness reports from Gran's somewhat spacy little neighbor ladies, particularly Triola, who was close to ninety. But Dottie was her grandmother's best friend and constant companion, and fear stabbed Allie at the thought that something might have happened to the dog.

A quick call to the police assured Allie that no help would be forthcoming from that quarter. The sergeant on duty, whom she knew, suggested that little old ladies should keep better track of their dogs. Obviously passing the buck, he referred her to the pound and to the prosecutor's office. "See if I ever call you when I need a cat out of a tree," she yelled as she slammed down the phone. Actually, the police had long since quit responding to her rescue calls. She was currently working her way through the fire department. She quickly called the pound and told them to be on the lookout.

Allie fumed as she donned her pea jacket and crumpled hat and started into town in the old pickup, using anger to mask her growing feeling of dread.

Cupid's Campaign   11

She was in rare form by the time she walked into the prosecutor's office. She knew damn well that Dottie wasn't lost. If her grandmother said Dottie had been stolen, then Dottie had been stolen. And that possibility made Allie even more afraid. She marched up to the young woman at the reception desk who seemed to be giving all her attention to a vampire-length fingernail. "I want to report a kidnapping."

The blue eyeshadow seemed to dance as the woman jerked her head toward Allie. "A kidnapping? I don't think we do kidnappings. I think that's the police." The inch long eyelashes fluttered.

"The police sent me over here."

"Oh." The young woman obviously hadn't had experience with such things, but she'd been in county government long enough to know how to pass the buck. "Maybe you'd better talk to one of the prosecutors. Second door on the right down the hall." Mission accomplished, she returned to her fingernail.

Allie stomped down the hall and threw open the office door without knocking, fuming that people wouldn't take a dognapping seriously. She opened her mouth just as the man looked up from his desk. She closed her mouth as she realized it was the man she'd encountered at the mall on Saturday. She stared into the deep blue eyes and saw recognition spread over his face. Recognition and something else. He looked a whole lot more formidable behind a desk than he had surrounded by animal lovers. He also didn't look very happy to see her as he stood up. Her mind raced and her heart pounded as she tried to think of something to say. "Hi. I'm here to report a kidnapping..." Her voice trailed off to nothing.

"A kidnapping. Have you been to the police?" His

rich voice held a note of amusement as his eyebrows arched.

"They sent me here. Actually, it's a dognapping." His voice enveloped her like a blanket of warmth.

"That figures." Frank stared at the young woman—faded jeans, surplus pea jacket, same ridiculous hat. Same rich auburn wisps framing the same satiny cheeks. Same eyes. But somehow the eyes were different today. The flashing green had been replaced by worry—fear, perhaps. Frank looked toward a chair and motioned her to sit.

He had no intention of getting involved in some frivolous animal business even if the business involved those enchanting eyes. He had important things to do. On the other hand, he *would* like to know who she was, and, from her wilted demeanor, he knew something had happened to her. He suddenly wanted to know what. Besides, they were in his territory now without an audience. "Would you like to sit down, Miss..."

"Allie Tarkington." She slumped into a chair, surprised he was even being civil after the hard time she'd given him on Saturday. She'd have to be nice to him if she expected him to help. Trying her best to ignore the warmth she suddenly felt, she wondered what approach would be best. Perhaps a little remorse would do the trick. She leaned forward and gave him her best helpless look. He probably liked helpless females. "It's Dottie. She's been kidnapped and Triola and Gladys think they saw the 'nappers."

Frank smiled at her obvious discomfort and tried in vain to follow the conversation. "Uh, you might want to tell me who Dottie is. Then maybe we could move on to Triola and Gladys." He was sure one of those names was the dog's but for the life of him, he couldn't figure out which. He wished to hell she'd quit looking so helpless. It was more disconcerting than her anger.

"Oh, right." Allie tried to pull her gaze away from his. She couldn't seem to think staring into those blue eyes. "Dottie is my grandmother's mostly Dachshund. She's missing. The other two are Gran's neighbors." Allie fanned her face with the wide lapel of the pea jacket. She couldn't imagine why anyone would keep an office so hot.

"I see. Well, have you looked for the dog? It probably wandered away." He stood and moved around his desk, pulling at his collar as he perched on the edge of the desk.

Allie watched as he moved to tower over her. Hoping she was making more sense than she felt at the moment, she hurried to explain. "Oh, no. They're inseparable. Dottie doesn't wander off." She suddenly reached over and grabbed his hand. "You've got to do something. There is a ring of dognappers in this area, preying on family pets. We've got to stop them." Her impassioned speech fizzled as she felt a jolt of hot current race up her arm and settle in her throat. Maybe it was static electricity from her wool jacket. Or had her heart jumped into her throat? She swallowed hard.

Frank's pulse quickened as he took her hands in his. He knew he should retreat to his side of the desk, but he wanted to touch her, see that she was feeling the same thing he felt. One look at those wonderful eyes told him she was. "Miss Tarkington, I'd like to help, but this office is involved in a number of very important cases right now, and, well . . ."

She snatched back her hands and jumped out of the chair, clutching them together as if they'd been burned. She knew she had to gather her wits about her and that didn't seem possible anywhere close to him. She backed toward the door until he was safely behind his desk again and then she summoned up enough anger to mask her feelings. "And you don't have time to waste on an old lady and her dog? Well, let me tell you something." She advanced on his desk and leaned over it, her face inches from his. "If you did more about animal abuse, there wouldn't be as much child abuse. If there wasn't so much child abuse, there'd be fewer murders. And if . . ." She caught a scent of some very expensive aftershave and felt lightheaded. The argument fled from her mind. "Please?"

Frank's eyes settled on the gentle curves of her sweatshirt as the heavy jacket fell open. He didn't want to get involved with this crazy woman, but something about her pulled irresistibly at a hidden part of him. He sensed an intensity he hadn't seen for a long time. She exuded a passion for what she believed in, a sincerity he found exciting. He wanted to do something. Maybe just file a report or something. "Well." He cleared his throat.

"Oh, thank you." She grabbed his hand again and felt another shock. "I'm sorry about Saturday, but you know how it is. Most people just don't care. And you being a lawyer and all, well. Anyway, we don't have time to run you through the tests to see if you're up to snuff. We'll just have to take you on chance. Come on. Gran and the crew are waiting."

"But . . . tests?" Before Frank knew what had hit him, he found himself following her out of his warm office and being hustled into a battered '56 Ford pickup. Somewhere along the way, he'd lost his home territory advantage. Wondering what else he would lose before the day was over, Frank had a sinking feeling that he was getting involved in something he would come to regret. Frank's mind raced along with his heart. He would humor her just long enough to find out why in hell she made him feel as if he were sitting on a high voltage wire.

Chapter Two

FRANK HELD ON to the rickety door handle as Allie careened through city streets paying little attention to stoplights and none whatsoever to stop signs. He could see the headlines—CANDIDATE FOR PROSECUTOR'S JOB AND ANIMAL ACTIVIST ARRESTED ON RECKLESS DRIVING CHARGE. He watched her, paying little attention to the ongoing commentary on the statistics of unwanted pets. She leaned forward in the seat, her short legs barely able to reach the pedals of the old truck. Her body was in constant motion, energy seeming to radiate from the small package. Although her legs were encased in faded denim, Frank knew they would be as perfect as the rest of her. At that thought, he quickly shifted his gaze out the window.

As they headed into one of the older, wealthier sections of town, he began to wonder why they were going in this direction. His consternation grew when she turned onto Jefferson Avenue, the center of the old historical section of Reedsville. He swallowed his surprise when she pulled into the drive of a turn-of-the-century

Cupid's Campaign 17

house complete with servants' quarters in the back. She wheeled the ancient truck to the back entrance. "Your grandmother lives here?"

Allie shot him a look of exasperation. "Where'd you think she lived? Sunrise City or some sordid place like that? Did you know they don't allow pets in nursing homes? But we're working on that."

Frank pondered the situation, hanging on to the door handle as the truck slowed, anxious to be out in the cold air again—away from the lemony scent and away from thoughts of... things. He found it hard to believe the woman driving the truck was related to anyone living in this mansion. But he was sure the little old lady living here was probably chairman of some political committee who would shoot him out of the election if he didn't find her damn dog. Well, he would just have to talk to the old lady, calm her down and forget about the whole thing. He extricated himself from the truck and followed Allie into the house.

"I have to park the truck in back. Gran says it's not good for the image of the neighborhood."

Before Frank could answer, he found himself in a kitchen big enough to feed the entire town. And faced with three little old ladies, one of whom was being consoled by the other two. Tears streaked her face, starting anew when Allie bent to hug her. The woman who must be Allie's grandmother was rather plump with silver hair, and Frank judged her to be in her late seventies or early eighties.

"It's all right, Gran. This is Franklin Wade. He's going to help us. Hi Triola. Hi Gladys."

Frank stared at the assemblage. Triola was old. Very old. And judging from the thickness of her glasses, damn near blind. Gladys was the youngster of the group, late sixties probably, wiry, bright-eyed, and covered from head to toe with silk and jewels which Frank was certain had not come from Woolworth's. He nodded to each lady.

Gran, who introduced herself as Elspeth Tarkington, dabbed at her eyes with a lace handkerchief. "Tea is ready in the parlor."

"Oh, Gran, you shouldn't have bothered."

"Now, Allison, we must remain civilized, even in the face of crisis." With a final dab to her cheeks, she led the group to a room filled with antiques and the elegance of days gone by. Thick oriental rugs accented the delicate cherry tables and chairs. Brocade and damask abounded.

Frank sat down in a Victorian rocker which his mother would have killed for, feeling as if he'd wandered into the twilight zone—or the set of *Arsenic and Old Lace*. A rotund little woman wafted in carrying a tray laden with a teapot and various and sundry goodies which she set in front of Elspeth. She sniffled loudly as she left the room.

"Bernice is quite upset," she said, indicating the cook-and-housekeeper's retreating back. "She's been with me so long I'm afraid she's almost family. I trust India tea will be acceptable, Mr. Wade."

"Fine," he replied confidently, although he wasn't much of a fan of the beverage. He would have preferred coffee—preferably laced with brandy to deal with his shock. He accepted the china cup and smiled at the ladies, wondering what was next on their eccentric agenda.

Frank's mind worked on a plan. He would inspire a little confidence in the legal system, make his excuses, and go back to what he'd been doing when those jade

Cupid's Campaign 19

eyes had so rudely interrupted his life. Gladys sat on his right, Allie on his left, Elspeth and Triola across the gleaming cherry coffee table. He was surrounded. He smiled confidently, avoiding even a glance in Allie's direction, waiting for someone to say something.

Gladys solved his dilemma, laying a jeweled hand on his knee. "Mr. Wade, you simply must do something about this dog situation. First, Mrs. Symmington's Boopsie, then Martha's Oliver, now dear Elspeth's Dottie."

Frank nodded and bit into a cucumber sandwich, the first he'd ever tasted. He'd thought cucumber sandwiches existed only in British mystery books. "Yes, well, of course we'll do all we can. Which is not very much. You see, the prosecutor's office is not really an investigative office." He began to relax. These were reasonable ladies, they would see he was not in a position to solve the mystery. "It's really a police matter."

Allie piped up. "Frank, uh, Mr. Wade, doesn't have a dog, and he doesn't think animal problems are top priority, Gran." She sat back, smugly sipping her tea, then munching some disgustingly gooey chocolate concoction.

Frank shot Allie a sharp glance just as she set her plate down and whipped off her ratty hat. An unbelievable amount of rich auburn hair cascaded down past her shoulders, and he stared at her, his tea forgotten, a cucumber sandwich frozen in mid-air. It seemed impossible for that much hair to tumble out of that silly hat. "I didn't say that. Exactly." Gladys pressed more cucumber sandwiches on him, ignoring the one in transit to his mouth.

"Well, you weren't exactly bubbling with enthusiasm

over Dottie." Allie resumed eating, licking the chocolate from her fingers.

Frank watched, fascinated, as her tongue flicked over each finger in turn. His pulse raced as he tried to remember why he was there. Allie looked up from a finger and her eyes met his. She shifted nervously, then focused her attention on her tea cup. "I didn't think..." The cucumber sandwich caught Frank's attention and he disposed of it in one bite, angry with himself that he would allow her to get to him like that. It was time to take charge. "Mrs. Tarkington—"

"Children, please. Now, Mr. Wade. Dottie has been stolen and I not only want her back, I want her kidnappers punished to the full letter of the law. Triola, you'd best tell him what you saw."

Triola's eyes wandered around until they zeroed in on Frank's left shoulder. "Well, it was quite frightening. As you may or may not know, Mr. Wade, this is a very close-knit neighborhood. We watch out for one another. Anyway, I'm a rather poor sleeper. That happens when one gets old, you know."

Gladys set her tea cup down with a tinkle of fine china. "Triola, this young man is not interested in the infirmities of old age. Get on with the story."

Triola bristled. "Well, really, Gladys, I'm just trying to fill in a little background. I would hate for Mr. Wade to think I dreamed this. Anyway, I looked out the front window and saw a truck, like Allison's but rather newer I think, creeping down the street. It was exactly three a.m."

Frank interrupted, deciding the better part of valor would be to get the story over with and get the hell out of here. He seriously doubted that Triola could even see the street, let alone a truck. "Do you know what kind of

Cupid's Campaign 21

truck?" He shot a glance at Allie to let her know he was taking things seriously, then did a double take when he realized she was staring at him, her gooey chocolate concoction forgotten. He smiled, certain now that she was not immune to whatever seemed to be going on between them. At least *that* was a consolation of sorts.

Allie sighed and focused on Triola. Her voice had dropped into that husky range again. "Of course she doesn't know what kind of truck. The only truck she's ever seen is mine and the gardener's. One doesn't own trucks on Jefferson Avenue." She sat twisting a lock of hair around one finger, refusing to even look in his direction.

Frank's eyes sought her once again, unable to concentrate on anything at that moment except her lovely hair and and those exquisite eyes. She belonged in silk, not rags.

Gladys tapped him on the knee. "Well, a truck on our street in the middle of the night is rather sinister, don't you think? I'm certain it was the one who stole Dottie."

Elspeth spoke up. "Of course Dottie has her own doggie door, so I didn't miss her till this morning. And some mornings she does like to play hide and seek for her morning treats. Most naughty of her, of course."

Frank gave her a sympathetic smile, hoping the ladies were hard of hearing. Otherwise, they would surely hear the pounding in his chest. "Of course." He looked around at the expectant faces. "Well, uh, what did you want me to do? I think this is a matter for the police."

Allie gave him a look of total disgust. "The police are not interested. Now, the ladies think there is a ring operating in this town. Probably selling the dogs to that lab over in Dunbar. I know a lot of people who have had pets stolen, so I agree. The police may well be a part of it."

She smiled and leaned closer to Frank. "So, you've been elected to help. You may not be quite up to par on animal issues, but your vibes are good, so you must be honest." Getting no response, she leaned closer, and the warm feelings she'd experienced flared to raging heat. "Besides, you're running for office. Breaking up something like this could be a big plus for your campaign."

Frank was drowning in a sea of jade green, but mention of his campaign made him sit up and take notice. That was all his campaign needed—a big dognapping case. He could see the headlines now.

"Oh, is he running for office?" Elspeth asked. She listened quietly to Allie's explanation. "Well, of course I'm not actively involved in politics since Mr. Tarkington passed on, but I could speak to Herbie."

Frank groaned audibly. She could only be talking about Herbert Atchley, the head of the party's State Committee. Which meant, if he didn't find the damn dog, he could forget about any political future. With a sigh of resignation, he pulled a little notebook from his breast pocket. This was not going to be as simple as he'd thought. "A Dachshund, you said?"

Elspeth smiled. "Mostly. We think she may have a little German Shepherd in her."

"Dachshund and German Shepherd?" Frank stopped writing, his mind temporarily boggled at the logistics of creating that particular mixture.

Allie placed her hand on his knee, then snatched it back. "We rescued Dottie from the pound. Some twit of a woman tossed her aside because she ate the bark off the rhododendrons."

Frank tried to ignore the tingling in his knee where

her hand had touched him. Why couldn't Dottie have been a rare breed from Outer Mongolia worth millions? He could see himself wasting the taxpayers' money over a mongrel. "How much would you say she's worth?"

All the women grumbled in unison. "How can you possibly set a value on something beyond value?" Elspeth wailed, breaking out in a fresh round of tears. "Of course I'm still hoping for a ransom call."

"A ransom call?" Perhaps this really *was* a set for the *Twilight Zone*.

"Well, it's better than thinking of her in that lab, young man," Gladys said indignantly. "After all, if they kidnap children for ransom, why not Dottie?"

Frank rose to his feet, not wishing to contemplate the intricacies of ransoming a dog. It was bad enough contemplating all the blank spaces he would have in his report—like value and pedigree. He couldn't even justify grand larceny. "Well, ladies, thank you for the tea. I'll do what I can. Have to get back to the office." He waited for Allie to follow, watching as she hugged her grandmother.

"I'll make sure he stays on it, Gran. 'Bye, ladies."

Frank climbed into the old truck and slammed the door, angry that he'd been neatly herded into a corner by a bunch of little old ladies; more angry that this flower child chattering beside him had hit him like a ton of bricks. But as the lemony scent invaded his nostrils once more, he knew this woman was not the flaky flower child he'd thought she was. There was something more...

"I'll take you on a tour of the neighborhood, Frank, kind of give you an overview of who's got dogs and who's missing dogs. The 'nappers will be back for more, you know. You're not from Reedsville, are you?"

"No, I'm from Lamar." Lamar was a neighboring town some ten miles to the north. "And I don't want to go on a tour of the neighborhood, I want to go back to my office. I have important things to do."

Allie reached over and laid a hand on his arm. "Frank, this *is* important." She dazzled him with a smile. "Besides those three ladies are an awesome force in this town. If they set their minds to it, they'll shoot you right out of the water in your campaign. Herbie used to mow their lawns when he was a kid. They baked cookies for him."

Frank's political star flashed, then fizzled before his very eyes. He wanted to shake her. Then he turned to see her tucking all that hair into that ridiculous hat. His hand reached for an errant strand, then stopped. "That's blackmail."

She abandoned her hair and fought to get the lumbering truck turned around. "Of course. Little old ladies are perfectly capable of it. They also hold grudges."

Frank gripped the door handle as the truck rattled out onto the street. Always a confident, self-assured man, he felt as if he'd been transported to never-never land. He peered out the window, looking for the Cheshire Cat he knew must be grinning down from one of the stately oak trees lining the avenue. "There's really nothing I can do. I don't have any investigative staff. We just prosecute people who have already been arrested." Dammit, Frank's life was well-organized and carefully planned. He knew where he was going—at least he had until today.

"No sweat. I'll do the legwork. You just find out who in the power structure is involved. There must be someone. That's obviously why we can't get any action."

He couldn't believe the nerve of the woman. "What

Cupid's Campaign 25

am I supposed to do? Drop by and ask the police chief if he's involved in stealing dogs?" Frank unbuttoned his coat and wished she'd turn down the heater.

"Well, I think you need to be a little more subtle than that." She pointed out a huge ante-bellum house surrounded by a tall wrought-iron fence. "That's where Boopsie lived."

"How nice for Boopsie. Will you have dinner with me?" Frank heard the words, but didn't believe he'd said them.

"Oh, I can't this week. I have some orphans who have to be fed at six and medicated at eight."

"Oh." Frank felt relief and disappointment at the same time as he tugged at his collar.

"But you could come to my house." She turned to him, ignoring the fact that the old truck was headed for the curb. "I have a few animals. You don't really despise animals, do you?" She wrestled the truck back into the street.

"Of course I don't despise animals. I've just never been around them much. My mother didn't like animals around." Frank felt himself slipping deeper and deeper into those wonderful green eyes. He turned away. Just his natural curiosity, he thought. He would find out who she *really* was, why she'd devoted her life to animals, then he could forget about her and get on with his campaign and work. A simple, logical course.

"Well, there you are."

"Where?" Had he missed something?

"Deprived, Frank. We're talking serious deprivation. But we can take care of that." She wheeled into the county courthouse parking lot and scribbled some directions on the back of an envelope. "Come at six."

A blast of cold wind hit Frank as he opened the door,

ripping away the warmth and lemony smell of the truck cab, bringing him back to his senses. He'd call her later, give her some excuse. He wasn't just about to get tangled up with some flake whose life revolved around animals. And he wasn't going to be blackmailed by a bunch of little old ladies. Stalking into his office, he felt his confidence returning. He'd just been temporarily overwhelmed by a beautiful woman in never-never land. As he started reading a brief on a robbery case, his door opened.

"Frank, I need to talk to you." The man framed in the door was in his mid-sixties, gray-haired and rotund, his ample stomach offering clear evidence of his sedentary life and his love of food and drink.

"Sure, Max." He waved at a chair. Max Gilbow was the county prosecuting attorney. The man who'd brought Frank in five years before as an assistant prosecutor. The man who had groomed Frank to take over when he retired. Frank had known early on that he wanted to be prosecutor, so he'd made it a point to never really lock horns with Max, but he would secretly be glad when Max retired. Max was of the old school of politics, and Frank suspected there were favors and deals cut that the rest of the staff never knew about. A practice that would stop when Frank became prosecutor.

"That woman who just dropped you off. Do you know who she is?"

Caution crept over Frank. "Some woman whose grandmother's dog was stolen. She thought I ought to do something about it."

"Hmm."

"Why?"

"Well, stay away from her. She's trouble."

"Oh?" Frank decided to play dumb. "How so?"

"She's a fanatic. Given the city and county lots of trouble about animal ordinances and such. Crazy. If she had her way, we'd spend all our time chasing after people who don't feed their cats like they're supposed to. Anyway, be bad for your campaign if people thought she was a supporter."

"Oh." There seemed nothing else to say on the subject of Allie. Frank wasn't about to try and defend the person who at the moment was turning his well-ordered life topsy-turvy. "By the way, Max, have you heard anything about an organized group stealing pets to sell to labs?"

Max jumped up and waved a stubby finger at Frank. "See? She's already got to you. That rumor starts every time some old lady misplaces her damn poodle. No, there is no such ring. Never has been, never will be. Take my advice, Frank. Stay away from her." He stomped out of the office.

Frank leaned back in his chair, tapping his chin with a long, strong finger. Why had Max been so vehement about a simple question? Maybe there *was* something in what Allie had said. Frank's curiosity was piqued, and Frank seldom let curiosity lie around untended. He usually found answers. He'd go to Allie's house and find out a little more about her suspicions.

He pushed aside any thoughts that maybe he just wanted to see her again, to find out what made her tick. It was strictly business. He had been pushed into a corner and he was going to push his way right out again. Frank returned to the brief, but his mind kept getting sidetracked to the question of how her hair would look in the bright sunshine of summer. He could almost see the burnished golden highlights.

Chapter Three

FRANK ARRIVED AT a rambling old farmhouse on the outskirts of town promptly at six. Obviously Allie didn't have access to her grandmother's money if the condition of the house was any indication. It looked somewhat run-down, but as Frank climbed the steps, he decided it wasn't as bad as it looked—it mostly needed paint. Actually it had a certain charm that seemed to fit the woman who lived there.

His knock on the door elicited a din of barking from behind the house, and Frank waited as visions of the Hounds of the Baskervilles raced through his mind. He hoped to hell that whatever was out there was chained or penned or something. His mood was not improved by the howling and scurrying sounds on the other side of the door. He heard Allie scream, "Back, Chevy," and hoped the creature was not so named for its size. Just as he considered canceling the whole crazy idea, the door opened.

Allie stood, a scraggly kitten in each arm, a very large German Shepherd captured between her leg and

Cupid's Campaign 29

the wall. She wore a kelly green sweatsuit. A green scarf held most of her hair in a ponytail, but errant wisps drifted and curled around her face and slender neck. Frank's fingers itched to untie the scarf and free that gorgeous hair. His eyes took in the soft curves beneath the sweatsuit, curves lost under her usual work shirt. His eyes stopped when they reached the slavering dog.

"Come in, Frank." She shifted one kitten to the other arm to open the storm door. Seeing his concerned glance at the dog, she smiled. "Don't worry, he won't bother you." With that, she started down the hall.

Having prosecuted a number of dog bite cases involving family pets who "wouldn't hurt a fly" but who had gnawed someone's ankle off, Frank didn't believe for a moment that the huge dog would not bother him, but her action gave him little choice. He followed her. As soon as he stepped into the house, the dog began howling and nibbling on his fingers. He froze. "Uh, you're sure he won't bother me?" he called to the retreating figure.

"I'm sure, unless you're not a nice person. Then he gets funny. Come on, Chev, cookie time." The dog bolted for a door at the end of the hall, almost upsetting Allie and the kittens in the process.

Frank fought the urge to take his person, pounding heart and all, right back to his car and go home. He wasn't at all crazy about the idea of having his character judged by a giant canine. He suspected "funny" as applied to the dog meant gnawed ankles rather than funny ha-ha. But he followed, finally ending up in a huge room that seemed to be a kitchen and living area. The old house looked like something out of a country living magazine, but with the added clutter of an assortment of aquariums, cages, toys, and creatures. It was a drastic change from Frank's neat, sterile apartment. He leaned against the wall as the canine consumed a huge dogbone in seconds.

"I'm feeding the kittens. Have a seat." She set each kitten on the floor before a bowl of murky liquid, which the kittens began to lap enthusiastically. The huge dog stood over them and drooled.

"Aren't you afraid he'll eat them?" In spite of his intention to get to the bottom of her suspicions about the kidnapping and leave, Frank found himself more curious than ever about Allie.

"Who? Chev? Why would he eat them? He loves babies."

Frank was afraid that meant he only ate grownups. "I don't know. Aren't dogs supposed to not like cats or something? They chase cats."

Allie sighed and looked up from the kittens. "Prejudice and ignorance. He just consumed a gallon of Purina Dog Chow. You see, Frank, you automatically associate *canis lupus* with *canis familiaris*."

"Canis whatus?" Frank gazed into her eyes and felt that now familiar quickening of his pulse.

"Oh, Frank, you do have a lot to learn. Wolf, Frank. If Chev were a wolf out in the wild, he'd probably eat the kitties. Wolves have to survive. But he's a domestic dog. Domestic dogs eat dog food, not kitties."

"Oh." Why did he feel like a second grader? Damn it, he'd seen plenty of pet dogs chase things and kill them. "Are you going to tell me he wouldn't kill a rabbit if he caught one?"

"Well, of course he would if it were outside. He's not *completely* domesticated. But he damn sure wouldn't

Cupid's Campaign 31

touch one hair on a bunny's head if I brought it in the house."

Relieved he wasn't facing this woman in a court of law, Frank decided a change of subject was in order. "His name is Chevy?" He watched her closely, noting her graceful movements as she bent to stroke the kittens. Gentle curves beneath the soft sweat pants made his heart thump against his conservative white shirt.

Allie laughed. "His registered name is Chivas Regal of Pinecrest, but the name lay heavy on his head. You know, animals feel responsibilities, too. He just felt he couldn't measure up. So it got shortened to Chevis, Chevy, Chev, whatever. Part of the time it's Dammit— as in Dammit, Chev." She squatted down and picked up the kittens, snuggling one against each cheek.

Frank smiled at her description of the big dog and watched her gentle touch with the tiny creatures. As he surveyed the scene, a strange warmth seemed to spread over him, a warmth he'd never experienced before. And it was something deeper than the physical warmth he'd felt earlier in the day.

She stood up and gently tucked the kittens into a cat bed in the adjoining room and quietly shut the door. Chevis stood at the door and howled as if his world had ended. Allie turned to Frank. "Now, about dinner. Is spaghetti okay?"

"Fine. What can I do?" He felt comfortable sitting in the jumbled kitchen, watching Allie mother her little charges. His pulse had settled down to a gentle racing simmer, but his curiosity grew by leaps and bounds as he wondered how she'd gotten so involved with animals. In spite of her brashness, he sensed a warmth and gentleness and surmised that she felt more comfortable with them than she did with people. He wondered why. He also noticed her occasional sideways glance at him.

"Not a thing. This is a microwave special. Wander around and get acquainted. Shut up, Chev. You can visit your kitties when they have their pills." As he stood up and started into the living room, Allie turned and gave him a long look, her eyes taking in his navy slacks, white shirt, tweed sport jacket and the shock of dark blond hair that would have been unruly in a strong wind. His features were handsome—a little bit rugged, but not too rugged, she thought as she watched him scan the living room. "Well, you haven't bolted and Chev didn't eat you, so there may be hope for you yet."

In spite of the strangeness of the house, Frank felt remarkably relaxed. He didn't know if it was because he felt a considerable fascination for Allie, or if he was just relieved that Chevis *hadn't* eaten him and seemed to show no inclination to do so. He preferred to think the latter, but strongly suspected the first. "Should I have bolted?" His deep, rich voice took on a silky quality as he turned to watch her.

Allie shrugged and put a dish in the microwave. "Most men do. Men can't seem to get in touch with their feelings when it comes to animals. They have to show dominance and aggression. I have to tell you, I don't particularly like lawyers."

"Any particular reason?" Curiosity flared. Lawsuit? An old love? What?

"Plenty. I'll show you the aquariums." She joined him in the living area where four lighted tanks lined one wall. A rainbow of colors flitted through the tanks, and she carefully explained each one to him, including one which held strange-looking crabs.

Frank stood close to her, breathing in the freshness of

Cupid's Campaign 33

her hair and the faint lemony scent he'd noticed the first day. He'd never smelled anything like her lemon scent, but he loved it. She turned toward him, and for a moment their eyes locked and Frank had an irresistible desire to kiss her. Her eyes took on a deep, mossy green shade in the dim light and Frank's blood started to simmer again.

The microwave bell caused her to duck under his arm and scurry to the kitchen. He took a deep breath, wondering what the hell he was doing there in a veritable zoo, thinking about kissing the woman who ran it. He'd been so sure she was just a little bit crazy. Now he knew it wasn't craziness, it was a deep commitment to something she believed in—the kind of commitment so rare these days. The same way Frank felt about the law.

Frank wandered around the room, stopping to look at a number of original watercolors and shelves full of delicately carved animals and birds. The room had a warm, lived-in look and feel. He finally stopped in front of three cages on a shelf near the kitchen. All he could see of the occupants were beady eyes peering out from piles of cedar shavings. He walked back to the kitchen, not sure he wanted to know what the eyes were attached to. He'd never seen so many animals under one roof and he suddenly wanted to know—needed to know—why this woman surrounded herself with them. "Uh, where did you get all the animals?" Surely she did something for a living.

"They're all rejects." Her eyes flashed with anger as she put plates on the table and brought out a bowl of salad from the refrigerator.

"Rejects?" Frank felt her anger as he watched her clear creamy skin flush.

"Dumped animals, stray animals, animals that were

cute when somebody got them, then grew up and weren't cute anymore, so they didn't want them." She stared squarely into Frank's eyes as she moved toward the table and him. "It's a vicious world out there for fur persons, Frank."

Frank's admiration for her took a quantum leap, fueled by the intensity of her statement and the fire in her eyes. The women he dated weren't that intense about anything, not even their daddy's money. "I never knew." Her face was now inches from his and he felt a crackling charge flowing from her. He wanted to hold her close, absorb the anger and fire, soothe her with a gentle kiss.

"Of course you didn't. No one does. No one cares. That's the problem." She felt her anger fade into something else as she stared at him, lost in the blue eyes, the salad bowl forgotten. She wavered, a warm flush burning her cheeks.

"I care." He cared about everything concerning this woman suddenly. His hands covered hers on the sides of the salad bowl as the aroma of Italian dressing wafted up.

She flipped her head, causing the ponytail to swing, brushing his cheek. Her words mirrored her intensity, but her voice dropped to a husky softness, her whole being caught in those flickering, blue eyes. "Oh, you say that, but do you really? I mean, do you care when it comes down to taking them home with you? Cleaning the litter pans?" She leaned even closer, freeing one hand so she could tap his chest. Not poke, just tap—almost caress—the white shirt front. "Frank, there are twenty homeless dogs in the backyard."

Frank gasped as her finger touched him again, then captured it in his hand, savoring the vibrant warmth and softness, ignoring the dangerous tilt of the salad bowl. "Twenty?"

"Twenty. Do you still care?" She pulled her hand free and laid it flat on his chest.

"Of course." Frank felt a sudden urge to take all twenty dogs home, along with their mistress.

She turned, breathing deeply, and put the salad on the table. "No, you don't. Not really. But you will when I get through with you." She flashed him a mischievous grin, followed by a look of total solemnity as her slender hand wiped her fevered brow. "Chevis likes you a lot and he's a good judge of people. I'm going to teach you to care, Frank. I think you may have it in you."

Frank felt as if he'd been handed a solemn trust to guard, but then he would have cherished any teachings she cared to give. He could only nod as they sat down to eat.

They consumed a vast quantity of salad and pasta and retired to the living room with coffee. Frank took an antique rocking chair and Allie sat on the sofa, legs curled tightly under her. Two cats immediately materialized from nowhere and settled on her lap after giving Frank indignant looks. Allie absentmindedly stroked them. "Now, about Dottie."

Frank sighed, knowing the subject had to come up sooner or later. "Nothing. I talked to a couple of people and they haven't heard of any dog-theft ring."

"They're probably part of it. Well, what are we going to do?" She stroked one cat's head.

"Allie, isn't it possible Dottie wandered off?" Frank didn't want to talk about Dottie, he wanted to talk about how she was going to teach him to care. Not that he didn't already care, but... his mind wandered to cool forest glades and moss and...

"Certainly not. Dottie doesn't wander. She's devoted to Gran."

"Isn't it possible Triola imagined the truck?" He went through the questions as he watched her delicate hand gently ruffle the cat's fur.

"You don't know those ladies. Nothing goes on in that neighborhood they don't know about. If she said there was a truck, there was a truck. Gladys did some calling this afternoon. Five dogs are missing from that neighborhood. We've got to stop it. Do you know what happens to animals that go to labs?"

At that moment, Chevis launched himself toward Frank, ending up with his front legs wrapped around Frank's neck, alternately licking and howling. Frank froze, stoically awaiting the fatal bite.

"He really likes you. He doesn't usually care too much for men. Chev, go find a kitty." The dog immediately flung himself toward the sofa and began frantically nuzzling the cats, who seemed to take no notice of the huge slobbering dog. "We'll have to stake out the neighborhood, Frank."

Frank wiped drool as inconspicuously as possible from his white shirt. At least the huge slobbering dog had dragged him back to reality, away from the forest glade. "You don't even know there are thieves. Besides, I can't go around staking out things. The police stake out things, I go to court. I have murderers and robbers to prosecute, a campaign to manage. The primary is just around the corner."

Even as Frank made all the excuses, he knew he would end up huddled on a street corner somewhere with this woman, freezing to death. In spite of himself, his prosecutor's mind was busily rifling through the possibilities of a ring of thieves operating with the knowledge, if not the approval, of some city or county officials. But he just wasn't about to admit any of those possibilities to Allie. *I thought that's why you came tonight—to get information.*

"Remember Herbie, Frank." She shifted nervously under his intense gaze.

"How could I possibly forget Herbie," he said with resignation. He wanted to allay the suspicions she'd generated, but for himself, not for Herbie and not because he was being blackmailed by a bunch of little old ladies.

"Time to give medicine, Chev." The hulking dog gave the cats one last nuzzle and bounded to the kitchen where he started howling again. Allie motioned for Frank to follow.

In minutes, Frank found himself holding two kittens while Allie administered pills, followed by some foul looking liquid which they seemed to love. Her hand brushed his time and time again. Between the warmth of her hands and the purring of the soft, furry kittens, Frank began to feel warm and lightheaded. A previously unfelt male protectiveness surged through him as he participated in the nurturing. When she looked up at him and reached for the kittens, he leaned down and kissed her. Her lips were as soft and warm as the kittens.

She responded for a long moment, hands against his chest where she had reached to take the kittens, eyes closed, heart pounding. A kitten mewed softly and Allie stepped back and retrieved the kittens, her eyes wide. She stumbled backward until she bumped into the kitchen counter, clutching the kittens so tightly one finally squalled in protest. Her mouth opened and closed several times before words would come. "Frank, I think... I mean, we better stick to business." Her eyes flashed green as a spring morning.

"I didn't mean to do that, but..." Frank felt a momentary confusion over the intensity of his feelings and the obvious effect on her as his heart raced along at a marathon rate.

"I have to see to the kitties," she mumbled as she put more distance between them, placing the kittens on the floor for Chevis to wash and turning to the sink. "Uh, you haven't been around animals much, have you?" A stupid question, but somehow she couldn't think of anything else.

"No. My mother didn't approve." Frank wanted to kiss her again, but sensed it would be a mistake to push her. Besides, he was having enough trouble dealing with his own reeling senses. When she turned back from the sink, he could see she had recovered her composure, but Frank felt a surge of excitement. She had felt it. Oh, had she felt it—exactly what he had felt, judging from her flushed face. She stood composed and cool, but that flush and the dark swirling in her eyes told him what he wanted to know.

"Ah-ha. Well, we'll have to remedy that. In the meantime, I'll case the neighborhood for the best stake-out and let you know."

"Allie, I think we'd best find some proof of some sort first." Frank couldn't believe he was agreeing to her hairbrained scheme. But inwardly, he knew he was agreeing so he could see her again. One kiss had not begun to answer his questions about this woman—it had just created more questions. Until his curiosity was satisfied, he would be unable to forget her and her menagerie.

"We will, Frank, we will." She grinned at him. "Trust me, Frank, you're doing the right thing."

He sighed and tried to smile. "Why don't I believe that? I'd better go." Frank still reeled from the sensation of the kiss. He needed to get some fresh air and figure out what he'd wandered into. Whatever it was, it felt very nice. "Good night."

"Good night. Sure you don't want to take a kitten or puppy home with you?"

"Not tonight." He stepped onto the porch and sucked in the cold air, hoping to clear his head, but it didn't seem to help. He drove home in a daze with visions of auburn hair, jade eyes, and soft silky lips parading through his mind.

Frank decided a cold shower might help and headed for his bedroom as soon as he walked in the door. Undressing, he noticed white cat hair all over the seat of his wool trousers and studied them before tossing them to the floor. He'd never in his life come home from a dinner date with cat hair on his pants. He looked around the room. Why did his place look so damn sterile and un-lived in? It never had before.

What in the hell was he doing getting involved with a woman who had a house and yard full of animals? Not to mention the fact that she seemed intent on treating him like a second grader who needed basic training in pets. Now that distance and the cold night air had restored his composure, he could see the absurdity of the whole thing. She might have wonderful eyes, hair he longed to run his fingers through, lips as sweet as nectar, but she liked animals better than people. How could he get involved with someone like that? Herbie. That's how he could get involved.

* * *

Allie cleaned up the kitchen and wandered into the living room, wondering what had happened to her. Every time she got near Frank, she felt warm. Then he'd kissed her and the warmth had turned to molten fire. And he was a lawyer. Allie had sworn she would never, ever even get close to another lawyer.

Allie sighed and tried to push back the sudden loneliness that swept over her. It didn't happen often, but her work was emotionally draining and sometimes she just needed someone to share with, someone to hold her and wipe her tears away. Because pain and tears were part of who she was and what she did. She had often thought sharing would delay the inevitable professional burn out, but she had given up finding a man who shared her love of animals. Well, there *were* some, but somehow they always turned out to be even weirder than lawyers. At any rate, she would have to put up with this one till they found Dottie.

But she would have to keep Frank away from her mother. If her mother got a whiff of an up and coming young politician, Allie would never have any peace. Allie smiled. Speaking of her mother, she'd better let her know about Dottie. Not that it would register with her mother, but it seemed the thing to do. She dialed and waited. "Mother?"

"Allison, what a surprise. Run out of pitiful creatures to tend to?"

Allie ignored her mother's jab about her chosen occupation. "Mother, Dottie was dognapped. Gran is very upset. You might want to see her tomorrow."

"Tomorrow? I'll tell your father."

"Daddy is in New York for the week, remember?" Allie couldn't believe her mother was so out of it. "How can you forget that? Don't you even notice when he's missing?"

"Oh, of course. Well, he does travel a lot. One simply loses track, dear. But tomorrow is out of the question. I have a tennis tournament in the morning and bridge in the afternoon. She can get another dog. I'm sure you have plenty to spare."

"Mother, she's upset."

"Well, she's your father's mother. *He* can call her." Jane Tarkington had never gotten along too well with her mother-in-law. Actually, she was intimidated by Elspeth.

Allie fumed. "Well, send Lisa over there." For all the good that would do. Lisa was Allie's older sister and took after their mother more than their father. Allie was convinced she and her father were the only sane ones in the family. Lisa was staying at home between marriages. Two months in New York playing second fiddle to a starving artist had been too much. Allie thought she was currently looking for an orthopedic surgeon.

"Oh, I think she's going to the lake tomorrow with the Fergusons. Something about hoping to sprain her ankle on water skis, but I may have misunderstood."

"I doubt it. Well, later, Mother."

"Allison, when are you going to be through this animal phase of yours? You simply must get yourself together. It's gone on much too long. Your father wants grandchildren before he dies."

"Mother, he's only fifty-two. Let Lisa have them."

"Poor Lisa. You really need to talk to her, Allie. She's having a terrible time."

Allie didn't want to hear about Lisa's terrible time. Lisa was basically a nice person, but she just refused to have anything to do with reality and growing up.

"'night, Mother." She hung up the phone. Her family was one of the wealthier families in the area, and her mother enjoyed all the perks of that wealth. Her only wish for her daughters was to see them well-married and with a houseful of darling little brats. Well, not Allie. She had found her calling in life. And it was to take care of homeless and forgotten fur persons and teach children to respect animals. That was all she needed to make her happy. Well, maybe she could teach Frank a few things, too, about caring.

Chapter Four

ALLIE COULDN'T FIND a parking place anywhere near the courthouse the next morning, so her mood was not the best when she finally arrived at Frank's office. She'd spent a restless night. Every time she'd dozed off, she'd seemed to drift into the kitchen again, reliving the kiss which had shaken her right down to the tips of her toes. Allie couldn't remember the last time she'd felt that warm fuzzy feeling slip over her whole being like a down comforter. And with a lawyer, of all people.

She'd finally abandoned her bed at the crack of dawn and sat in her living room drinking strong coffee and watching the aquariums. They usually made her feel tranquil, but this morning, the electric blue on the tiny neons reminded her of Frank's electric blue eyes.

She would *not* let herself get involved with him. Involvement would mean distraction from her work. It would result in having to make a choice at some point between further involvement and her animals. It would mean warm, fuzzy feelings instead of warm, fuzzy puppies, it would mean... Allie abandoned her coffee for the crisp morning air of the backyard, lecturing loudly to the dogs, all of whom seemed agreeable to whatever she said.

She finally abandoned them, arguing with Chevis that she didn't even know why she was thinking about future decisions. There was not going to be any future with Frank. She would do what had to be done to gain his cooperation in the matter of Dottie, but that would be it. Period. Chevis didn't seem to care about her dilemma—he was much more interested in the possibility of getting another dogbone. She abandoned him, thinking her animals should be a little bit more sympathetic, considering what she'd done for them.

This time she knocked at Frank's door before bursting in, thinking he might be more amenable to the stakeout if she were polite. She had decided he tended toward staid and conservative, and she didn't want to just keep overwhelming him. When she opened the door in response to a muffled "Yes?" she found herself looking right square into those electric blue eyes and began to wonder who was overwhelming whom. "Hi." She stood just inside the door.

He rose and came around the desk, smiling and motioning her to a chair. "Good morning." She noticed he had shed his jacket. The white oxford cloth shirt fit him like a second skin. A burgundy tie lay across his desk. Allie's eyes went to his throat. Blond hair curled around the open collar. She gulped and wondered what his bare chest would look like.

Allie felt his eyes follow her as she hurried to sit down. She waited for him to go back to his chair but instead felt him come to stand behind her. She could almost feel the heat of his body.

Cupid's Campaign 45

"What can I do for you this morning?" His voice held a soft note of amusement.

Allie craned her neck around to look at him, taking in the flat expanse of white shirt which seemed to fill her field of vision. She looked higher, but curling hair and eyes and things were up there. "I found a stakeout," she said weakly, turning back to face his desk.

He leaned over, his hands on the back of her chair. "And you just dropped by to order me to be there tonight. Right?"

Why didn't he go back to his side of the desk? Allie got the definite impression that he wasn't overwhelmed anymore, but maybe it was just because they were on his territory. She wished she'd brought Chev. Chev was very good at keeping people overwhelmed. "I thought I'd drop by and tell you. You know, just in case you were in the neighborhood and wanted to help or something."

He leaned closer until his lips were inches from her ear. "Just in case I might be in the neighborhood, huh?"

Allie felt the soft puff of breath on her neck and shivered, scrunching further down into her pea jacket. "Just in case." She felt him shift his weight and sighed in relief when she realized he was headed back to his desk. As he sat down, she noticed the smile on his face. A smile which Allie thought smacked very strongly of a smirk. His eyes danced with barely concealed humor. Just because of one lousy shiver on her part, no doubt.

"Allie, I am not going on a stakeout with you, because *you* are not going on a stakeout." He waited for the words to sink in. "If there is any staking out to be done, it's a matter for the police."

Allie frowned out from her collar. "I might have known you'd be just like the rest of them."

"And what's that supposed to mean?" He put his elbows on the desk, fingertips steepled in front, eyes squarely focused on her—eyes from which the humor had gone.

"I had high hopes for you, Frank, but I guess you're in it with the rest of them." She slumped down in the chair. She knew she wasn't being fair to him, but maybe if he got mad enough, he would help.

Frank's hands slapped the desk and he leaned toward her as far as he could, half rising from his chair, eyes flashing. His voice had a hard edge to it. "You think whatever you want of me personally, Miss Tarkington, but don't you ever accuse me of being involved with anyone or anything illegal!"

Allie sat up in her chair, surprised at his reaction. She hadn't really meant anything like that, but if she wanted him mad, she'd obviously succeeded. "I didn't mean you kidnapped Dottie or anything. I just meant..." What had she meant? The more his eyes flashed, the deeper the blue became and the wider her own eyes grew in response.

Frank glared at her for a moment, then leaned back again and took a deep breath, knowing he had over-reacted. But he couldn't stand her thinking he might do something unethical. "Okay, I know what you meant. But you don't have a shred of proof that Dottie was stolen. You don't have a shred of proof that a ring exists. Allie, the law works on evidence, not speculation on the part of one young woman and a bunch of little old ladies."

"You just don't want to get involved." Why was she picking at him? "I understand, I guess," she admitted grudgingly.

"No, you don't. I *can't* get involved. There's nothing

Cupid's Campaign 47

to get involved in. You can't just go running around spying on people and following them and those sorts of things. There is a constitution in this country, remember?" Frank just wasn't about to forget the constitution, even in the face of dejected, jade-green eyes. He didn't want to argue with her. He wanted to...

Allie leaned forward, her arms on his desk. "I don't want a course in constitutional law, Frank. I want some help finding Dottie."

Frank sighed. "Allie, go to the police. Tell them what you suspect. When they catch someone, I'll be more than happy to prosecute them fully. I want to help, there's just nothing I can do." He couldn't possibly jeopardize his campaign for a mongrel dog and a woman who made his pulse race.

She grinned, sensing a bit of waver in his voice. "You could help me stake out the neighborhood."

"You haven't heard a word I've said, have you?" Frank knew it had come down to a matter of her telling him where to meet her. He couldn't seem to say no to those incredible eyes.

"I heard it, I just hoped you didn't believe it. Frank, we only have five more days."

He frowned. "Why do we only have five days?" And why didn't she accept no for an answer?

"Because a week is how long they usually hold the dogs before they ship them out. That's why. Then poor Dottie... well, what they do is worse than death."

"Dammit, Allie, you're trying to blackmail me, just like your grandmother. Do you know what would happen if the police knew I was out doing their job?" No more Mr. Nice Guy. Time to get tough. Assistant prosecutors didn't take cases based on eyes and scents and racing pulses.

"No, but I'm sure you could handle it, Frank." Her voice spoke of candlelight and soft music.

"Well, just forget it." He picked up a brief, determined to ignore the pleading in her eyes.

Allie stood. "Just in case you're out tonight, Frank, I'll be on Jefferson, near Walnut. Just in case." She started toward the door.

"I'm working tonight." He refused to look up, sensing that the sadness in her voice might be reflected in her face and he couldn't stand that.

"Oh." Allie shrugged. "Well, just in case." She hiked back to her car fuming—fuming that she'd been such a wimp. She should have demanded that he help. Fuming that he caused the strange sensations which no doubt were responsible for her uncharacteristic weakness.

Frank spent the afternoon in court prosecuting a drug dealer. His case was well prepared and a conviction resulted, but somehow, Frank didn't feel that exhilaration he'd learned to love after a successful case. Allie Tarkington had danced around the edges of his mind all afternoon, and during the celebration drink after court with other members of the office, he could think of little else.

Frank didn't like all these strange new feelings which had intruded on all the old familiar feelings. He'd put a dangerous man behind bars, so why wasn't he feeling the usual high? Why was he worrying about that strange woman with lovely hair and flashing eyes? Except that each time he saw her, she seemed less strange and more beautiful. Frank returned to his office and threw himself into his work.

He finally gave it up at eight o'clock and headed home, stopping for a hamburger on the way. For some reason, he didn't want to go home to his neat apartment. And when he finally got there and changed clothes, he felt a restlessness akin to what he felt on the day of a big case—a tingling anticipation. He paced the floor, he sat and turned the pages of a law journal without seeing a word, he put on his coat, got in his car, and screamed out of the parking lot. And headed for the historical district, cursing all the way, half the words aimed at himself, the other half aimed at the woman he searched for.

He drove slowly through darkened streets fronting stately old homes until he saw the truck. He parked some fifty yards behind it and sat watching it, reluctant to take that final step which would lead him to the old truck and Allie.

There was no sign of life in or around the truck as Frank watched, and worry began to nibble at his mind. What if she was right? The street lay in deserted quietness, the only sound his harsh breathing. It would be the perfect neighborhood for dog thieves—the residents were mostly widows, and no one was out on the street after dark. Frank's nerves felt stretched to the limit as he waited for some sign of life from the old truck. What if something had happened to her? With a final expletive, Frank left his car and sprinted to the silent truck. He rapped softly on the back swing-up door, his heart pounding.

"Come in, Frank," a muffled voice called.

Frank breathed a sigh of relief at the sound of her voice, but anger flared when the words soaked in. He jerked up the door. "How the hell did you know it was me?" His eyes strained to adjust to the darkness.

"Because you're basically a decent person, Frank. The tailgate doesn't work very well. In fact it hardly ever works, so you kind of have to climb over it." She knelt in front of the opening, peering out at him.

Frank managed to roll over the nonfunctioning tailgate with a modicum of grace and found himself sitting on a mattress which covered the entire floor of the truck bed. As his eyes adjusted to the pale light streaming in the camper windows from a streetlight, he saw the bank of equipment and gadgets on one side. "What is all that?" He recognized most of it, but didn't believe it.

Allie shifted to give him more room. "Surveillance equipment." She waved a hand toward the equipment. "Infrared camera, tape stuff, spy mikes, the usual."

"I don't believe this. What are you? The Mata Hari of Reedsville?" From never-never land to *Miami Vice* in one easy step. He managed to bump his head as he maneuvered himself into a sitting position. Since his head was already ringing, he hardly noticed.

"Frank, when you're tracking down animal abusers, you have to have the proper equipment." She sat across the truck from him, chin resting on her knees, arms drawn tightly around them.

"It looks more like you're tracking down Russian missile bases. Good Lord, Allie, you could run the police department in New York with all that stuff." She didn't just *care* about animals, she was equipped to track them down and compile evidence which would stand up in a court of law. A grudging admiration nibbled at Frank. It was too dark to see her clearly, but he imagined the curve of her hip beneath the tightly stretched jeans.

She smiled. "Sometimes I loan it to the one here. Would you like some coffee?" She stretched toward a box.

"Sure, why not? Everybody drinks coffee while

Cupid's Campaign 51

they're on stakeout." He assumed the box contained survival rations—maybe a machine gun and a few hand grenades. He accepted the steaming mug, glad to have something to do with his hands besides throttle the woman now sitting Indian fashion, her knees almost touching his. He didn't even want to consider how ridiculous the whole scene must look. At least it was too dark to see her eyes. But of course darkness did nothing to mask her scent and the sound of her soft breathing. It just made it worse.

"Frank, this is serious business." She started to say more, but a rustling and soft mewing erupted from a pile of down comforter near the front of the truck.

"Don't tell me. You brought the kittens. I guess you keep them warm by the old flame-thrower." Frank thought any number of terrorists would love to get hold of this haul.

"Well, I couldn't just leave them at home. They have to have their food and medication on a regular basis." She scooted closer to the kittens, then turned to give him a strange look. "Why would I have a flame-thrower, Frank?"

Frank smiled to himself. She felt the heat, too, judging from her retreat to the kittens. "To go with all the other paraphernalia." He shed his jacket and leaned back against the wall of the camper, stretching his long legs so that she had to scrunch up against the kittens' bed if she didn't want to touch him. Maybe he could put a little pressure on her and she would leave him alone—forget about his help.

"Frank, I'm a pacifist. I don't shoot people or anything, I just gather evidence." She waved at the equipment. "Believe me, this is essential equipment."

He grinned in the darkness. "No hand grenades tucked under the kittens?"

"You're acting very strange tonight, Frank."

"Just an overactive imagination." He sipped at the coffee, watching her faint outline take on detail as his eyes adjusted to the dimness. "If you're so hot to trot on animal-abuse cases, why haven't I prosecuted any of them?" He would get to the bottom of this woman before the night was over. Frank shifted nervously at his choice of words.

Allie looked at the kittens instead of him. "Because your boss is an insensitive jerk."

Frank had thought the same many times, but wasn't about to admit it to her. "Really?"

"Really. It's almost impossible to get even a search warrant in this county, let alone a conviction. He won't even consider our cases."

Frank searched his mind for animal cases since he'd been in the office and couldn't remember any. Of course, some of the other prosecutors might have handled them, but he would have remembered some discussion in staff meetings. He didn't like the idea that something could have slipped past him. He liked her accusations about Max even less. "Maybe we just have a gentle populace."

"Don't kid yourself. We get most of our convictions in adjoining counties. My only hope for this county is the kids." She moved the comforter.

"Like the kids at the mall?" He watched her take a kitten from its bed and snuggle it in the hollow of her throat. It mewed softly as she gently rocked it. Frank struggled to keep up the conversation as feelings of warmth and gentleness swept over him.

"And the kids at the schools." She handed him the kitten. "Can you hold her for a minute?"

"Where do you teach?" Frank shifted again, this time a little closer to her, gently rocking his kitten. Its sweet smell mingled with Allie's, its tiny claws kneaded at his bare neck. Strange feelings brought a shiver to his body and a gentle touch to his heart.

"I go to all the schools. Like a traveling medicine show. We're trying to teach the kids responsible pet ownership." She gently popped a pill down the kitten's mouth, then let it lap from a tube of something.

"I had no idea the schools had such a program." He watched her cuddle the kitten against her cheek for a moment, then put it back to bed. She reached for his kitten, her hand brushing his cheek as she took it. She cuddled the kitten and repeated the process of pills and feeding. Frank stared, fascinated. Soft fur against a satiny cheek...

"They didn't until I convinced them they needed one." Allie didn't bother to add that they still wouldn't have one if her grandmother hadn't funded it and used a little push to convince the school board of the need.

So that explained what she did for a living. It still didn't explain how she could afford all this expensive equipment. But right now, he didn't care. His head was filled with the scents of kittens and lemon. "So what do you do when you're not out teaching or rescuing animals?"

Allie jerked her head sharply toward him. His voice had taken on a different quality—one which made her feel as if she were about to melt and run out the broken tailgate of the old truck. "Nothing."

Frank sensed her sudden discomfort, glad to have

company. His body felt like a tight wire, stretched to the limit. "Nothing at all?"

"Nothing at all. This keeps me busy."

"Allie, if you keep moving, you're going to be sitting on those poor kittens." He'd never realized how small the bed of a pickup really was.

"Well, you take up a lot of room," she said defensively.

"I could leave," he said in a quiet voice.

"I didn't mean that." She ducked to look out the window as a vehicle passed.

"Do you really think the dognappers are coming back?" He pushed himself up to more of a sitting position and leaned forward to look out the window, his face close to hers.

"Of course they will." Allie turned and felt his cheek brush hers. He didn't move. She thought she could see the vein at his temple thumping away. "So, are you going to run for governor when you've finished a term as prosecutor?" Allie wondered why she'd snagged that question out of the blue. But it was better than asking him if he was really wearing an after-shave called MALE, because that's what she kept smelling.

"Attorney general. Then, who knows?" His hand moved to her cheek, tilting her face until the streetlight picked up the soft jade in her eyes. "Why?"

His fingers burned a trail from Allie's cheek to the center of her being. "I just wondered. Gran says you have a bright political future. Will you be tough on the animal abusers?"

His lips brushed her cheek. "I will if you'll have dinner with me."

Allie retreated toward the kittens with the speed of a crab at high tide. She didn't want to have dinner with

Cupid's Campaign   55

him, she just wanted him to help find Dottie and prosecute the dognappers. At least that's what she thought she wanted. "I think I'm busy on stakeout every night. Except tomorrow."

"How about tomorrow?" He wanted to follow her, but contented himself with resuming his place against the camper wall.

"Well, I think we're having dinner with Gran. You and I."

"You and I? Dinner with Gran?" That was definitely not what he had in mind.

"She likes you a lot. She can help with your political campaign. She knows everyone. And with your bright future and all . . ."

"Like Herbie?" How had he gotten himself cornered so neatly? Dinner with *Arsenic and Old Lace* was a far cry from dinner by candlelight.

"Desperate situations require desperate measures, Frank," she replied softly.

Frank thought he'd never been in a more desperate situation than the one in which he currently found himself. Desperate to hold this woman, desperate to kiss her until neither one of them could breathe. "No doubt. I had in mind something more like a private dinner at a nice quiet place. Candlelight, wine."

"But the kittens."

"We'll take them with us. I know the owner." He would even take the twenty homeless dogs if necessary. To hell with the owner. Frank came to his senses when he heard a sharp rap on the camper door. He looked at Allie, but she just shrugged and retreated to the kittens —and the hand grenades.

"Anybody in there?" a gravelly voice called.

Frank sighed and slid over to the door. He knew who

that voice belonged to and his mind raced as he thought up and rejected plausible stories. He popped the door open and grinned at Ken Villines, the police chief of Reedsville. "Hi, Ken."

The burly, middle-aged man's eyes quickly scanned the scene. "Well now, Frank. You, uh, doin' some investigatin' or somethin'?" Allie's head appeared beside Frank. "Miz Tarkington." The chief nodded at Allie.

As Frank started to speak, Allie piped up. "We're doing your job, Chief."

Frank thought about elbowing her, but rejected it. "She didn't really mean that, Ken. What she meant was that we're just helping out a little." Frank felt Allie jab him in the ribs. Obviously she had no reservations about elbows. "It's just to make Mrs. Tarkington feel better about her dog."

Allie leaned out of the door. "Bullfeathers. We're doing what you're supposed to be doing, Chief. If you were out tracking down the dognappers, we wouldn't have to."

The chief grinned. "Yes ma'am. Well, we got a call that there was a strange truck parked here, and when one of the old ladies calls, I got to check it out myself." He grinned at Frank and shook his head. "Well now, I wouldn't want to disrupt an important investigation by the prosecutor's office." He gazed pointedly at the mattress.

"Actually, I'm not investigating anything, Ken. I'm just giving the young lady some advice on *her* investigation." Frank started to scramble out of the truck, then stopped. Falling out of the truck would be worse than staying where he was. He'd just have to convince Ken he was there on business. "We try to serve our constituents, you know."

Cupid's Campaign 57

"Well, that's real neighborly of you, Frank. Real neighborly." The chief headed for his car, his heavy shoulders shaking with laughter.

Frank scrambled out of the truck and whirled on Allie. "Now look what you've done."

"What have I done?" She hung part way out of the truck.

"This will be all over town by tomorrow," he hissed in a loud whisper. He could see his campaign drowning in a sea of laughter.

"So what? Do you really care what people like Ken think of you?"

"When you're in public office, of course you care."

"Well you shouldn't. That's what's wrong with our whole system."

Frank wasn't about to get into a discussion of the political system. Besides, he'd been raised to worry about what other people thought. More to the point, Ken had just thought Frank had been doing what Frank had wanted to do all evening. Guilt was not something Frank bore well. "Go home, Allie."

"I won't. I have a job to do."

"Then do it by yourself." He stalked toward his car, wondering what in the hell he was going to say to Max in the morning.

"Don't forget tomorrow night. Seven o'clock," Allie called after him in a loud whisper that echoed through the quiet streets.

Frank headed home. Damned if he would show up for dinner at the funny farm tomorrow night or any other night.

Chapter Five

ALLIE STAYED CLOSE to the front windows of Elspeth's living room, pretending to water the profusion of plants that grew in the spacious, airy room. She was so nervous she kept dribbling water on the walnut and cherry tables, then she would have to dash back to the kitchen for paper towels to mop up the mess before Elspeth saw it.

She was afraid Frank would *not* show—and perhaps more afraid that he *would*. She'd realized she hadn't been very sensitive last night. Of course, that was a recurring problem for Allie when she was in the midst of a crusade. Usually it didn't bother her, but it did now. Actually Frank Wade bothered her a lot in ways she was not used to. She wouldn't blame him if he didn't show. After all he was right. Public servants did have a public image to maintain. Which was why Allie preferred to fund and run her own show. That way, she was accountable to no one but herself and the animals.

She dribbled the last of her can of water on a porcelain plate instead of the African violet sitting on it and

Cupid's Campaign 59

dabbed with a worse-for-wear paper towel. She heard a car turn into the driveway and hurried to the window. She couldn't see the driver but recognized the red sports car. Taking a moment to smooth her carefully brushed hair and dab a bit of water from her nubby green wool slacks, she took a lot of deep breaths to calm her racing heart, then strolled toward the back of the house, wondering why he hadn't parked in front. She'd watered all those plants for nothing. Gran would not be happy if she'd drowned them.

Bernice was opening the back door as Allie entered the kitchen. Her breath caught in her throat when she saw him. He seemed to fill the kitchen with his presence. A soft knit vest had replaced the usual tailored pin stripe, a muted gray tweed jacket had replaced the suit coat, picking up flecks of gray in his blue eyes. She realized with a flash that strong, lithe muscles rippled under the tweed.

In each hand he held a slender bud vase containing one long-stemmed red rose. Before she could speak, he handed her one of the vases and smiled. Allie's hand trembled as she took the vase. No one had ever in her whole life given her a long stemmed rose. The other lawyer had been into daisies. She thought it was a silly thing to do—at least she'd always been pretty sure it was a silly thing to do.

"Where is your grandmother?" The deep velvety voice wrapped around her.

Allie waved toward the dining room, her bud vase clutched tightly to her breast. "Thank you." She tried her best to think of a snappy comeback, but none would come. At that moment, Elspeth sailed into the kitchen, balancing a half dozen old-fashioned salt cellars.

"Bernice, you forgot the salt cellars, dear."

Bernice turned from her sauce at the stove. "Oh, Miz T, nobody uses those things anymore. I put out the silver shakers."

"I like the old ways, Bernice." As the crystal cellars tumbled from her hands onto the counter, she looked up and smiled at Frank. "Good evening, young man. Oh, you're the young man who is going to find Dottie, aren't you?" She put a finger on her jaw and tapped her foot on the floor. "I must talk to you and Allison about something."

Frank handed her the rose. "For your kind invitation to dinner."

Elspeth flushed, a hand fluttering to her ample bosom. "Oh, my. No one has given me a single rose since Mr. Tarkington passed on. How lovely of you." She turned to Allie. "Your young man does have potential, my dear. Much more than that strange young man who had to do with chickens."

Frank watched Allie turn red. "Chickens?" He addressed his question to Elspeth.

Elspeth smiled angelically. "I can't recall just what now. But he was a bit strange. Of course, I always think people who try to exist on a diet of steamed soybeans do become strange, don't you?"

"Gran, we'd best get on with things." Allie tried to herd Elspeth toward the dining room, ignoring Frank and his wide smile.

"Not that I have anything against steamed soybeans, of course, but I do think one needs a balanced diet of meat and vegetables to develop properly. It was most wise of you not to marry that young man, Allison." With that, she hurried into the dining room.

As Allie tried to follow, Frank caught her by the arm. "Steamed soybeans?"

Cupid's Campaign   61

"He was into vegetarianism." Allie looked toward the ceiling as if help would be forthcoming from that quarter.

Frank led her out into the hallway. "So where did the chickens come in?" Her flushed cheeks looked as if they'd been brushed by a summer rose. Frank's sharp intake of air caused her to look up at him.

"He was organizing a 'Save the Chickens' group, but I could never figure out exactly what he hoped to save them from." She clutched the rose vase, turning it in her hands. Frank was obviously enjoying her discomfort.

"And you almost married him?" He glanced toward the kitchen door and urged her farther down the dim hallway.

"No, I did not almost marry him. Gran jumped to conclusions. She has high hopes for great-grandchildren." She looked up into his grinning face, waiting for him to say something. "It was a phase. I was just helping him out."

He leaned close, trapping her between himself and the wall. "And what kind of phase are you in now, Allison?" He stroked her rose-brushed cheek with the back of his fingers, delighting in the smooth softness.

"None. I've been through all the phases." She heard the back door slam. "Oh, someone's coming. We'd better go." She ducked under his arm and hurried into the kitchen.

Frank stood in the hallway for long moments, waiting for composure to return. Why did it bother him that she had perhaps dated some chicken fanatic? Or anyone else for that matter. As his pulse slowed down to normal, Frank thought back to his conversation with Max, which was the real reason he'd come tonight.

He'd been about to call and cancel when Max

jumped him about Ken's story. Except Max hadn't been laughing, he'd been worried. Frank could tell by his nervous gestures. And *that* worried Frank—and made him very curious. A curiosity that leaned closer to suspicion as the day passed. Why should the episode, which Frank had to admit was pretty funny after he had a chance to think about it, upset Max so much? Unless Max had something to fear from Allie's persistent investigation.

Frank's train of thought was interrupted by Allie opening the door from the kitchen and motioning for him. When he stepped back into the kitchen, he was facing a young woman draped in silk and gold chains. Her hair was a lighter shade of red than Allie's but the family resemblance was unmistakable. Her tall, slender figure looked almost anorexic to Frank, but she wore class and wealth like a second skin. She smiled at Frank, and under the carefully made-up face, he suspected there lurked a spattering of freckles.

"My sister, Lisa," Allie said in a voice of resignation. "Frank Wade."

Lisa limped toward Frank, her hand out. "So nice to meet you, Frank."

"My pleasure." Frank noticed the elastic bandage encasing one ankle and glanced at it. He gave it a questioning glance.

Lisa's clear laughter filled the kitchen. "A little accident on the lake."

Allie smiled sweetly. "She's trying to capture an orthopedic surgeon."

"Don't be crass, Allison." She smiled back at Frank. "I hate to ask, but could you possibly help me into the dining room?"

Before Frank could offer his arm, Allie glared at him

then confronted her sister. "What the hell are you doing here, Lisa?"

"I'm here to comfort dear Gran. Mother told me about Dottie. Poor thing." She latched onto Frank's arm.

Allie kicked the wall and addressed Bernice's broad back as Frank and Lisa disappeared into the dining room. "I'm going to kill her someday. Comfort, my foot. Just because the orthopedic surgeon turned out to be sixty and a grandfather, now I suppose she's into lawyers."

Allie stopped cold as she realized that what she was feeling was jealousy. Quickly brushing the thought aside, she refused to consider it further. Lisa always brought out the worst in her. She banged into the dining room to find Lisa rearranging the seating so that Allie would be across the table from Frank, who would now, conveniently, be sitting next to Lisa.

Elspeth was busy beside the hutch. "Bernice is getting so forgetful these days. She forgot the napkins again." She handed damask napkins to Allie. "Oh, thank you, my dear. What is that twit doing here?" she whispered to Allie as she nodded in Lisa's direction.

"I thought you invited her." Allie glanced at the table. Frank was seating Lisa, which did nothing to improve Allie's mood. She didn't dwell on why a gentlemanly gesture bothered her so.

Elspeth shot Allie an indignant look. "Please, Allison, I haven't taken complete leave of my senses yet."

Allie sighed. She seemed to be sighing a lot these days. "It's probably my fault. I told mother." She felt Frank's eyes burning a hole through her sweater and into her bare skin in spite of Lisa's attentions and twitterings about her accident.

"Oh. Your father called this morning. The poor boy is in New York." Elspeth turned toward the table, then stopped. "That's what I was going to tell you and your young man. The phone call."

"What phone call, Gran?" Frank caught Allie's eye as she looked toward him. His eyebrow raised in a question. Obviously he wasn't as wrapped up in Lisa as he acted.

"Well, I'm not sure. I thought it might be a ransom call, but he never called back." Elspeth stood quite still, a frown wrinkling her face.

Frank was beside Elspeth in a flash, guiding her to a chair just as Bernice appeared with a large bowl of salad. He put a hand on Elspeth's arm as he seated her. "What exactly did the caller say, Mrs. Tarkington?"

Elspeth gripped the arms of her chair. "Well, it was very strange. I can't think why I forgot about it until just now. I tried to call Allison right afterward, but she wasn't home." She smiled at Frank. "One doesn't always remember as one used to."

Allie patted her grandmother's arm. "It's okay, Gran. Just tell us what he said." She shot a questioning look at Frank, who returned it with a shrug, then turned his attentions back to Elspeth.

"Well, I couldn't make a lot of sense out of it. It was a young man, but he didn't sound at all like the kidnappers one hears on the television." Elspeth took a sip of water from the crystal goblet by her plate. "He kept saying the strangest things. Of course, I don't hear as I used to. But he asked some questions."

Allie interrupted. "What kind of questions?" She knew there was no hurrying Elspeth, but she had visions of being there all night waiting for the first clue.

"Well, all about where I lived and what I did for amusement."

Allie looked up, her worry increased tenfold by the frown on Frank's face. "You didn't tell him, did you?" She knew phone calls were a standard ploy for casing the houses in this neighborhood. A robbery was just what they needed on top of a dognapping.

"Well, he hardly gave me the opportunity. Then he asked if I'd ever done something or other with my dog. I didn't quite understand the question."

Allie thought her grandmother must have gotten the conversation very confused. When she looked up at Frank, his frown had disappeared. The corners of his mouth twitched and his eyes sparkled. How dare he laugh at Elspeth. "And what did you tell him?" she asked gently.

"I simply told him I would pay whatever was necessary to get Dottie back. Then there was an ever so long pause. Then I told him what I thought of young men who kidnapped dogs. And he hung up." She clasped Allie's hand in hers. "Oh, do you think he'll call back?"

Allie smiled as sudden realization hit her. She couldn't look at Frank, knowing they would both laugh. "Gran, I think what you got was an obscene phone call." Relief swept over her. No robbers.

"I beg your pardon?"

"An obscene phone call, Gran. And no, I don't think he'll call back." She could have kicked Frank if she could have reached him. He was almost choking with the effort to control his laughter. It seemed important they not laugh. Her grandmother would be very upset when she understood what the young man had been talking about.

Elspeth beamed. "Do you really think so, Allison?

Wait till Gladys hears this. She'll be green. Triola had one of those calls only last year, but Gladys and I had almost given up."

With that, Frank burst out into laughter, followed by Allie. Frank shook his head. "Almost given up? You mean you wanted one?"

Elspeth's chin raised a notch as she turned dignified eyes toward Frank. "Of course none of us *wanted* one, but one should experience everything in life before one passes on, and one does hear so much about these phone calls each spring. Of course it's only March. The young man must have been quite desperate. At any rate, Triola was quite unbearable for weeks."

Allie dished up the salad and they sat down to eat, still laughing about Elspeth's phone call. Allie noted that Lisa managed to brush against Frank with every bite and she thought about kicking her soundly under the table. Just as she was about to deliver the killing blow, she looked at Frank, whose gaze she'd been avoiding up to that point, not wanting to watch him succumb to Lisa's charms. As their eyes met, a jolt went through Allie and she almost dropped her fork. His gray-flecked blue eyes looked hungry and Allie had a sinking feeling it was not for the roast beef Bernice had just set on the table.

"Would you be so kind as to carve, Mr. Wade?" Elspeth asked, then smiled at his nod.

"Of course, Mrs. Tarkington."

Allie quickly averted her eyes to the beef, hoping it would sprout wings and fly off or do something to distract her and everyone else, but it just sat there. Frank immediately took up the fork and knife and began carving, and Allie wondered how he could possible cut a roast without looking. She could still feel his eyes burning on her body.

"Frank, you simply must tell us about some of your murder cases," Lisa drawled, seeming to sense she was losing control of the situation.

Frank laid a thin piece of perfectly carved beef on Elspeth's plate. "Most of the murder cases are handled by the chief prosecutor."

"Oh. Well, I just have to tell you how much I respect you for being in public service. I'm sure you would be ever so wealthy in private practice. People would simple flock to someone like you." Frank quickly served the sisters and himself.

Elspeth accepted green beans from Allie and turned to Lisa. "Don't be such a twit, Lisa dear. Franklin is Allison's young man."

Allie almost choked on her beef. She sputtered out a "Gran!" and looked at Frank, who sat looking at her, a quirky grin his only reaction. A *smug*, quirky grin, Allie thought. What the hell had happened to the man? During the first few encounters he'd acted as if he were scared to death of her, now he looked as if he had proprietary rights.

Lisa leaned into Frank again. "Oh, Gran, you know Allie doesn't do lawyers."

Elspeth glared at her oldest granddaughter. "Lisa, please try to restrain yourself. Just because you've been to the city is no reason to bring their rude ways home with you."

Lisa dazzled Frank with a smile. "I've just returned from New York. Gran thinks it's a wicked city."

Allie started to point out that Lisa hadn't thought much of it either, but stuffed a piece of broccoli in her mouth instead. "Good dinner, Gran," she said, although Bernice had, as usual, killed the broccoli hours ago.

Allie suffered through the interminable meal, Lisa twittering, Frank watching Allie's every move, Allie trying to convince her stomach that food belonged there instead of whatever the hell was fluttering around down there.

Lisa laid a well-manicured hand on Frank's arm. "Allie, you simply must bring Franklin to dinner. Mother will be enchanted with him."

Allie could see complications arising at an alarming rate. It was only a matter of time before Lisa started talking about lawyers again. She jumped up. "Well, you'll have to excuse us, ladies. Frank and I are going over to Dunbar to raid that lab and find Dottie." One look at Frank assured her that she had temporarily wiped the quirky grin off his face. She started for the door, Frank hot on her heels once he'd graciously thanked Elspeth for dinner.

Elspeth waved as if they were off on a Sunday picnic. "Be careful, children, and if you find Dottie, bring her right back here."

"Right, Gran." Allie bolted from the back door before Frank could catch her. The argument that was sure to ensue would be better heard by the neighbors than by Bernice. She stopped beside her old truck and waited, studying the fender of Frank's car which was parked beside hers.

Frank strode up to her, silent and foreboding. "And just what was that all about?"

"What?" She scuffed a foot at the concrete drive and turned her attention to the red door of the little car.

"You know damn well what I mean. How could you

raise false hopes by telling your grandmother we were off to do a John Wayne raid on that lab?"

"But we are going to the lab." She was very aware of his strength and closeness—his scent permeating her whole being, even in the cold night air.

"We? We? Allie, *we* are going to do no such thing. It's called breaking and entering. It's a felony. You go to jail for felonies."

"Frank, we don't have any choice." He stood so close she had to lean back to look up at him.

He stood scrutinizing her for a time, his fingers beating a tattoo on the cab of the truck. "You're really serious, aren't you?"

"Of course. Why else would I say it?" She wanted to back away, but the truck seemed to be in her way.

He stroked her cheek with a gentle finger, his consternation suddenly replaced by something else. "Maybe because your dear sister was trying her damnedest to drag a few skeletons out of the closet."

"I don't have any skeletons in my closet." She scrunched down the side of the truck, but he followed.

"Really? Then why don't you tell me about your not doing lawyers?" His velvety voice mesmerized her.

"Nothing. I was engaged to a lawyer once." Allie vowed to provide Lisa with the need to see another orthopedist at the earliest opportunity.

"Does that mean you just don't like *him* anymore, or you don't like any lawyer anymore?" He placed a hand on the truck, trapping her.

"Maybe some of each. We really need to be going."

"Did I hear a closet door slam somewhere?" He took her by the arm. "Okay. We are going to Dunbar, but just so I can get a look at this place and so you won't do anything stupid on your own. We are going to do what is known in the trade as a drive-by. That's where you drive by and don't stop." He guided her to his car.

"But what if Dottie's there?" Even through her wool coat she could feel the warmth of his touch radiating toward her shoulder. She quickly got into the car.

Frank leaned down, his face very close to hers. "You won't know that unless she's put a sign out front. Remember the operative word. *Drive-by.*"

Allie slouched down in the seat. "Right. Good old drive-by." She smiled and wished the sports car was a little larger or that she was in the back seat. As Frank maneuvered the little car out of the drive, Allie glanced at his profile—strong and handsome. Her blood simmered away, keeping pace with her rapid heartbeat. It was going to be a very long trip to Dunbar.

Frank stopped at the street and reached across her to lock the door, his arm lingering in the vicinity of her chest.

Allie looked at him in alarm. "Why'd you do that?"

"Because if you lean against that door any harder, I might lose you. Fasten your seatbelt."

"We're only going to Dunbar, not the moon," she grumbled, but quickly buckled up as he reached toward her again.

"Seatbelts save lives, dear heart." He whipped the little car out into the street. "It's hard to believe you and Lisa are sisters."

"I've often thought that myself." Soft music came from a speaker near Allie's knee. She guessed he'd whip out the candles at any moment. At least Lisa seemed a safe subject. Maybe she'd better pursue it. "She takes after Mother."

"And you take after your father?"

She nodded. "Except I didn't inherit his knack for

Cupid's Campaign   71

making money. He's in investment banking and real estate and I don't know what else."

"And your mother?" Frank was determined to put her at ease.

"She's into spending all the money Daddy makes. Lisa is a big help."

Frank chuckled. "I'll bet. You two don't seem to get along too well."

Allie sighed. "It's not as bad as it seems. She's just been such a twit since she got back from New York. I guess it's the divorce."

"Ah. That will make one strange. Two of my sisters have been through it. One recovered, I don't think the other one will ever be normal again. She's retired to a farm to raise Ginseng."

"You're kidding." Allie laughed as she began to relax. It was comforting to know that Frank had an oddball in his family. "How many brothers and sisters do you have?"

"Five. All spread to the far ends of the earth. I'm the only one who stayed close to home. I just never saw the need to go looking for something when everything I wanted was right here."

"That's kind of the way I feel about this part of the world." For some reason, Allie felt a flush of contentment. Frank seemed to be happy with himself and what he did. He wasn't searching for that elusive something on the other side of the hill. She liked that in a man. She sighed happily until she thought about what she'd just thought about. What *was* she thinking about? Frank wasn't a man, he was a lawyer.

Through her suddenly muddled thoughts, she caught him watching her. That is, he *was* a man, too much of a man. The soft music and talk of family had lulled her into forgetting that he was just someone who was helping her find Dottie. The scent of his maleness penetrated her senses again and she squirmed nervously. She had to think of him as a lawyer and politician, not a man. No easy task, locked together in a toy car.

Frank moved his head slightly so he could watch her, sensing first that she had finally relaxed, but then had thought of something and become nervous again. Personally, his nerves would break soon if he didn't find a distraction from her presence in such close quarters. They would do a quick drive-by, he would break all the speed limits getting home, and he would have a cold shower and a stiff drink.

Chapter Six

DUNBAR WAS A wide place in the road some twelve miles from Reedsville. A Quickie Market appeared to be the only thing remotely resembling life in the small town. Frank slowed to the posted twenty-five miles per hour as they drove past a closed gas station and a miniature city hall which looked about the size of a very small office. He slowed even more. "Well?"

Allie looked his way, too busy being relieved that they had arrived to comprehend what he meant. "Well what?"

Frank slowed to a crawl. "I suppose you do know where this place is."

"I've never actually been there, but I know about where it is." She desperately tried to remember what she'd been told about the place. "It's called Animal Services. Some service they do."

"Great. Do you have any idea how many miles of dirt road this country has?"

"Don't worry, we'll find it." She peered out of the window to get her bearings. "Go on through town, then there's a blacktop road to the right." Allie was sure she could find it in the daylight, but somehow things didn't look the same at night. Particularly when one was distracted by flutterings and pounding hearts and such things.

"I hate to tell you, but we went through town while you were trying to make up your mind." He grinned at her and slowed the car even more.

Allie rolled down the window, letting the cold night air wash across her face. She couldn't seem to think, let alone find some place in the middle of nowhere. She saw a road. "Right there. Turn right."

Frank turned onto the side road. In less than a mile the blacktop ended. In another half-mile, the road ended at the edge of a creek. Frank stopped the car. "It's very clever of them to have the lab on a pontoon boat—for quick getaways. Or is it an underwater facility?"

Allie could feel her neck turn red. Why hadn't she read through her files before she came. Somewhere, on a scrap of paper, she had directions. *Probably because you weren't planning to come until Lisa started talking about lawyers.* "So we took a wrong turn. We'll find it." Allie was not at all sure they would even get turned around on this goat trail, let alone back out to the main road. She wouldn't look at Frank because she knew she would see that quirky, smirky grin.

"Right." Frank put the car in reverse and started backing up the washboard road, looking for a place to turn around. His arm was draped over Allie's seat as he turned to look out the back window. The little car jolted its way backward.

Allie studiously examined the dark countryside which consisted of an overgrown ditch bank and an occasional beer can. Why did he have to be so damned

Cupid's Campaign 75

agreeable? Why didn't he just get mad and go home? Allie had visions of them still wandering around on dirt roads when the sun came up, by which time she would be a total basket case.

"Had I known we were going into the wilderness, we could have rented a Jeep."

Allie thought they would never find a turnaround. She sat rigidly avoiding contact with the arm on her seat. Each time they hit a pothole, his hand touched the back of her neck and the jolt she felt was not from the pothole. Nor were her shivers from the open window. Much as she hated the quivering sensations, she loved them. *Oh, that makes a lot of sense.* She breathed a sigh of relief when they were headed back to the main road and Frank was looking forward instead of backward. "Try the next road."

"Ah, there's nothing I like better than a scenic drive in the dead of night." He grinned at her and drove onto the main road again. "You've never been to this place, have you?"

"Well, I didn't say I had. All you lawyers ever think about are details." He was enjoying this.

"Well, you must admit that location is a rather important detail. Are you sure it even exists?"

"Of course it exists. Turn left." She was tired of his patience and mania for silly details. She felt the car slow and begin to jolt again as they drove onto a dirt road that made the first one look like an interstate.

He turned a serious face to her, but the corners of his mouth twitched. "Well, this one certainly looks promising."

She wanted to tell him to just shut up and drive, but held her tongue. She was, by now, so flustered by the sensations he caused that she mostly wanted to go home and get away from him. Except she didn't really want to do that, either. "The kind of business they run doesn't depend on drop-in traffic. They..." She stopped as they rounded a bend in the road and found themselves a few yards from a locked chainlink gate. A high fence disappeared into the woods in each direction. Inside the fence, a gray metal building dully reflected the headlights. Frank backed the car up and pulled it as far off the road as he could before killing the lights.

Frank pushed back against the seat, hands gripping the steering wheel. A serious note replaced the teasing in his voice. "This is just great. A dead-end road."

"So much for the old drive-by," Allie said brightly as she peered out the windshield.

"No signs. This could be a garage or something, Allie."

"Shh." Allie heard a faint barking somewhere behind the fence. "I hear dogs." As their eyes adjusted to the dark, the faint moonlight began to give some detail to the building. "This is it, all right," she whispered.

"Why are you whispering?," Frank said in a loud whisper. "The place is obviously deserted."

"I don't know," she whispered impatiently and started to open the car door.

"Where the hell do you think you're going?" He leaned over and held the door tight.

"To look around." She leaned into the door, trying to ignore the tense muscles of his arm lying across her breasts. The door opened and she almost fell out.

Grabbing her arm, he pulled her back into the car. "Oh, no you're not. *Drive-by*, remember? This road is public property, that fence and all the land around it and inside it are private property."

Allie shook off his hand. She couldn't decide if her

Cupid's Campaign 77

heart was in her throat because of the potentially dangerous situation or because of Frank. She feared the latter. "Good Lord, of all the people I could have brought, why did it have to be a lawyer?"

"Probably because I'm the only one crazy enough to come with you. Now that we've had our scenic tour, it's time to go home." He leaned over, trapping her against the seat. "Unless you want to make use of this delightful pig trail and do a little necking."

The thought of necking with Frank sent a new round of shivers down her spine as his scent filled her head. Allie squirmed away from him and concentrated on the business at hand. "Frank, this is a business trip." Allie had already decided she would come back by herself tomorrow night when she could concentrate on the business at hand and not be bothered with Frank's endless details. What was a little matter of private property where Dottie was concerned? She was trying to think of some really snappy comeback when she felt him freeze and turn quickly to look out the back window. As she turned, she saw dim headlights flash on the trees behind them.

Frank swore. "Company. Just what we need. You see the problems of dead-end roads?"

Before she could answer, she heard the sound of a truck lumbering up the dirt road. And before she could ask Frank what they should do, his arms circled her and his mouth sought hers. Thinking he must be having some sort of fit, she started to struggle, then forgot everything as his lips found hers.

Somewhere in the outer consciousness of Allie's mind, a truck slowed, then rattled on, a gate clanked open, then closed. These sounds registered, but could not compete with the sensations sweeping through her body. Her hands found his thick blond hair and buried themselves, her lips opened to his, her body caught fire. Time stood still as sensation after sensation engulfed her. When his lips abandoned her and cool air touched her face, her eyes flew open. "Why did you do that?" she squeaked.

His lips nibbled at her nose, but his eyes were turned toward the building. "Two reasons. Bad guys never bother lovers, and I wanted to."

Allie struggled to sit up straighter as his words struck home. He hadn't meant it, he'd just been trying to convince whoever was in that truck that they were just using the road for a lover's lane. That thought brought a stab of disappointment to her. Maybe he hadn't felt what she did. As cold air flooded through the open window, her heart slowed and with an angry start she reminded herself why they were there. "What are they doing?" She looked toward the fence, trying to figure out a way to tactfully untangle herself from his arms.

"Nothing. And be still. We can't leave until they do or they'll be suspicious." His lips trailed fire down the tender flesh of her neck and throat.

"Oh." She gave herself to the fire of his kisses, determined to hold up her end of the charade. But charade quickly turned to something else as the fire spread to the very center of her being. When he raised his head and she could breathe again, she heard a door slam somewhere and dogs barking. Leaning her head out the window and gulping air to clear her head, she listened carefully. "I'm sure I hear Dottie," she whispered breathlessly.

"That's ridiculous. There's no way you could tell her from all those others." He pulled her back and nuzzled her throat.

"I can too. She has a very distinctive bark. Almost a howl." She heard another door slam and Frank pushed her down in the seat, his mouth seeking hers again. She could feel his heartbeat against her breast and she knew the whole world could hear hers as his lips nibbled the corner of her mouth, then moved on to tease her neck. Again, she was only vaguely aware of the slamming gate and rattling truck. Then only the wonderful sensations of fire and warmth. She slipped her hands beneath his jacket and marveled at the long sinewy muscles of his back. She felt him shiver and pull her closer.

Frank raised his head and looked out the back window. "We can stop now. They're gone. Unless you want to stay for a while." He smoothed the hair away from her face and struggled for control.

She looked up to see that smirky grin and almost threw him off of her, fighting the confining seat to get upright, smoothing hair and shirt and anything else she could find to smooth. In the dim light she had seen the hunger in his eyes and knew it reflected what he must see in hers. With all the dignity she could muster, she stuck her chin in the air and looked out the window. "One does what one must do where animals are involved." Her voice held more squeak than authority.

Frank burst out laughing, the rich sound echoing through the quiet night. "Spoken like a true Tarkington. And if that's what you want to believe, my dear, you just believe away." He pulled her to him and planted a quick kiss on her cheek, then started the car. "For myself, I rather enjoyed it. I never knew surveillance could be so much fun."

Allie fumed silently, clinging to the door as far as she could get from him. "You're insufferable. You know that?" So he had felt it, and now he knew she had felt it, too. She willed her body to quit running away with itself.

His rich laughter filled the car. "It was your idea. I just came along for the ride. Maybe we should come back tomorrow night."

"Never. Did you see who was in the truck?" It was high time they got back to business, although Allie missed the raging heat when her heart slowed to an almost normal rate.

"I was busy. I thought you were watching." He gave her a sideways grin, still teasing, but only to disguise his hunger and his efforts to gain control.

"I was busy trying to fight you off." She wasn't about to admit anything to him.

"Tch, tch. And I thought it was true passion." The grin faded. "Allie, I don't want you coming back here, do you hear?"

"Ah-ha." She shook a rigid finger at him. "So you admit that something might be going on and that it might be dangerous."

"I admit to nothing of the kind." He gestured toward the fence. "But this is private property and trespassing is against the law." Frank didn't want to admit to her that he'd seen a rough, unsavory face giving them the once over as the truck passed them.

"And I suppose you would take great delight in prosecuting me—sending me to the cotton farm for the rest of my natural life."

He laid a hand on her arm and spoke gently. "No, Allie, I would not take any delight in that or in anything else that might harm you."

Allie cleared her throat. His words had caused that warm, fuzzy feeling again—not a raging heat, just warm and fuzzy. "Well, then do something. I can't believe you'd let a little thing like trespassing interfere with the lives of animals."

"Dammit, woman, the law is a sacred thing. If I can trespass for what I consider a good cause, then what is to prevent the police or anyone else from trespassing on my property if they consider it a good cause." Frank felt his passion for the law begin to replace some of his passion for Allie and breathed a sigh of relief. He needed a distraction.

"It's not the same thing. Lawyers!"

"Of course it's the same thing. It just depends on who's defining what a good cause is. And I'm not about to open that can of worms." Frank concentrated on the argument, but the knowledge that her eyes were flashing that brilliant green did nothing to aid his efforts at composure.

"So Dottie just loses her vocal cords and goes off to die for the betterment of humanity, right?" How could he be so stubborn?

"No. We do it legally, by the letter of the law." In spite of himself, the lemony scent crept into his consciousness, along with the impact of her last statement. "Why would she lose her vocal cords?" he asked in a quiet voice.

"Because they 'de-bark' them," she said in a trembling voice.

Frank felt pain and anger wash over him. He didn't want to know why, although instinctively he knew. "Allie, you're putting me in a very uncomfortable position."

"Certainly less uncomfortable than the one those poor dogs are in."

Frank hit the steering wheel with one hand. "Dammit, you're asking me to choose between the law and

Dottie. We can break the law and rescue one dog or we can put all of them behind bars, but we can't do both. We need to build a case that will stand up in court."

"We don't have time," she wailed.

"Then we save those who will come later. But first, we have to have some reason for a warrant." Frank felt pulled apart. He was an officer of the court and bound by the law, but he was also a human being.

In spite of herself, Allie perked up. She had to think about shutting down the lab and just hope like hell they were in time. But Frank was going to help after all. Of course, it might take ten years if they did everything legally, but at least it was a start. "Like what?"

"We need a name, a license number, a filed complaint, something that will justify an investigation of the lab or of a person connected with the lab." He glanced at her. "I'll make a few phone calls—see if I can find out anything." Thoughts of Dottie disturbed him deeply, but he buried them as best he could. They just had to find a way to hurry up the legal process.

"Why the change of heart?" She was suddenly suspicious, remembering his ardent kisses.

"Legitimate businesses don't set up in the middle of the woods and conduct business after dark." There was a hard edge to his voice. And they don't mutilate little old ladies' dogs, he thought. A grim determination set Frank's handsome features in a frown.

Allie stared at him with new respect. He was the first man she'd come across in a long time who seemed to have such strong feelings about right and wrong. Not that his right and wrong were her right and wrong, but ...Reedsville loomed ahead, then they were at Elspeth's and he was saying goodnight.

"I'll talk to you tomorrow about the next step." He

brushed a quick kiss on her cheek and was gone, leaving her standing by her old truck, trembling fingers touching her burning cheek.

Frank took a quick shower, a little colder than usual, and rifled through some work. He couldn't get any information about the lab until tomorrow, so he shoved that problem into a compartment of his mind to be dealt with later and turned his thoughts to Allie Tarkington.

He'd known he felt a real attraction to her, one he didn't begin to understand, but when he'd kissed her in the car, his whole world had exploded. What had started as a ruse to keep someone from possibly kicking their brains out had quickly turned into a sensual experience the likes of which he had never known. The gentle kissing and teasing he'd indulged in with her had in no way prepared him for what he'd felt tonight. And Frank was not an inexperienced man when it came to women.

The thing most remarkable to Frank was that she'd felt it, too. And responded. Oh, had she responded. Frank's body felt a sudden warmth just thinking about it. He knew she'd been avoiding close contact with him and now he knew why.

All of which meant he was experiencing a monumental desire for a woman who didn't even vaguely resemble the women Frank usually dated. Although he knew she wasn't the flake she would have people think, she was still very different—intense, independent, outspoken. Frank knew it was purely physical, because his well-ordered, logical mind would never allow his disciplined, well-kept body to get seriously involved with someone like Allie Tarkington.

Shoving thoughts of her aside, he thought again

about the lab. He didn't know a damn thing about the place, but deep in his gut he knew there was something very wrong with the place and the people who ran it. And he would damn well get to the bottom of it. He checked his answering machine and sighed at the message from his mother—an account of her conversation with Max about the imminent ruination of his political career by associating with known fanatics.

Deciding his mother would still be awake, since she never missed Johhny Carson, Frank dialed her number. Better to get it out of the way now than to have her call at the office tomorrow. "Hi, Mom."

"Franklin, where have you been? Out with that— that fanatic person?"

Frank thought that if mothers could rig elections, he would be the youngest president the country had ever seen. "Mom, she's not a fanatic. Her name is Allie Tarkington and I'm just helping her with a little problem." No response. "Mom? Are you still there?"

"Franklin, is she one of *the* Tarkingtons?"

Frank grinned. Leave it to his mother to sniff out any possible money or social connections. "Well, her grandmother is, I'm not sure about her. I mean she's one of them, but I don't think she's got any money herself."

A series of strange gasping noises came over the phone. "Franklin, she's loaded."

"How do you know that?"

More gasping noises. "Everyone knows that. At least anyone who gets his nose out of his law briefs for a moment. Oh, I can't wait. When can you bring her to dinner?"

"Mom, I'm not dating her, it's strictly business." At least it might have been, more or less, until that kiss in the car.

"Well, get with it, Franklin. She'd be the perfect wife for a politician."

"A minute ago she was a fanatic, now she's a future wife. Which is it, Mom?" Frank grinned. His mother kept telling him people just didn't elect bachelor governors.

"She's probably just going through a phase."

"Good night, Mom." He hung up the phone, knowing he would never have any peace now. But his mind was on Allie. Why hadn't he figured out she had money after seeing Elspeth's place? He'd just assumed whatever money the family had was gone, like many of the old families in northern Mississippi. "Genteel poverty" was the phrase. So Allie was just masquerading as a simple little crusader for animals. Interesting. Amazing, actually, for someone who had grown up in the lap of luxury to devote herself to something as demanding and usually disappointing as animal rights work must be.

Then another thought struck him. What if it *was* just a phase? Would she change back into another Lisa? He'd been certain Allie belonged in silk, now he wasn't at all sure—about a lot of things.

Chapter Seven

FRANK SPENT MOST of the morning making phone calls, trying to get a handle on who owned the lab in Dunbar. The more calls he made, the more curious he became. When he finally discovered that several holding companies and dummy corporations were involved, his excitement surged—that same thrill of excitement he felt when he'd uncovered a crucial piece of evidence in a case. There was no question that a number of people were very anxious to hide their involvement in the lab, and Frank knew from experience that when people wanted to hide ownership, there was generally something more serious to be hidden.

He dialed Allie's number. Although he had no intention of telling her what he'd found, which to a layman wouldn't sound like much, he wanted to tell her enough to deter her from going off on some half-cocked trip to the lab in the middle of the night. Frank felt a stab of disappointment as the phone rang and rang. He was almost ready to hang up when a breathless Allie answered. He smiled at her husky "hello."

"Hi. Where were you?" he asked.

"When you have twenty dogs in the backyard, you have morning chores that go well into afternoon."

"Well, we're going to dinner tonight to give you a rest. I'll pick you up at seven." He held his breath, afraid she would refuse.

There was a long pause. "I don't know. I have—"

"I know. You have kitties. I promise to have you home no later than nine, which will be only an hour late for their pills." He could hear the reluctance in her voice and willed her to say yes.

"I thought we could take them with us."

"I don't really know the owner quite *that* well." He had caught the teasing quality of her voice and knew she would go.

"You certainly do take a lot for granted."

Frank chuckled, imagining her dilemma. His voice when he spoke again was silky. "After last night, I thought I was entitled." He heard a number of expletives explode in his ear.

"Nothing happened last night. It was all in the line of duty. And it won't happen again. Our stakeout team has been disbanded."

"Too bad. I was all ready to change occupations." Frank closed his eyes and saw her clutching the phone, a light rosy flush coloring her satiny cheeks. His pulse quickened.

"Ohhh . . . men," she sputtered.

The silky voice turned teasing. "Well, if you're sure nothing happened last night, and if you don't like our wonderful surveillance teamwork, I guess there's no need to tell you what I've turned up this morning."

"What? Tell me." Her voice reflected some hope and a lot of doubt.

"Well, since we're not a team anymore..." He could see her rigid stance—half hope, half fear—and knew he shouldn't tease her. "It's mostly good news. At least it isn't bad."

She almost sent a big raspberry through the phone. "Are you going to tell me or do you want to tell Chevis? I could tell him you're not a nice person, you know."

"Chevis loves me, remember?" Frank had heard the relief in her sigh when he mentioned good news, so he could withhold his meager information. Otherwise, she might not go to dinner with him.

"Augh."

"Augh?"

"That's the nicest thing I can think of to say right now."

"Look, I'll tell all at dinner tonight. No dinner, no information." He checked his watch. Why hadn't he insisted on a late lunch? Dinner was many hours away and he wanted to see her, reassure her that they were making some progress.

"That's blackmail."

He laughed. "I know. One can learn a lot from little old ladies. See you at seven." He hung up before she could reply, smiling. He was beginning to like that quickening pulse she caused. He was also beginning to suspect that he needed it more than he cared to admit.

He leaned back and stared at the work on his desk. As he picked up a brief, his eyes caught one of his bumper stickers lying on the desk. Which brought him to another problem—his campaign.

He hadn't done any campaigning since Saturday. He'd have to get back in gear. If he could recruit more campaign workers, they could do a lot of the work and he could get to the bottom of the dognapping thing. He

Cupid's Campaign 89

toyed with the idea of recruiting Allie and her family. Except that raised other nagging thoughts. Allie was hardly the kind of person he envisioned as a campaigner. But with the Tarkington name, the whole family was bound to be well connected. Hmm. He would have to think that through. There was little doubt that Elspeth and her crew would go all out if he found Dottie.

A new and disturbing thought hit him. What if her reluctance to get involved had to do with her money? Perhaps it was not only the lawyer, perhaps she had tired of people putting the touch on her. Perhaps she was afraid that he would ask her for a contribution...

He opened the brief, suddenly not too anxious to follow that line of thought, his mood visibly altered. What he felt for Allie was a high-voltage physical attraction, which he would satisfy if at all possible. Period. Which had nothing to do with his campaign or the Tarkington influence or anything else except a physical need. So why was he thinking in terms of the future with Allie? And why was he worried that she might worry about her money? None of it made sense. Their association would probably end when the problem of Dottie was resolved. He immersed himself in the brief, refusing to pursue his uncomfortable introspection.

Allie sat pressed against her side of the car on the way to the restaurant. She'd been waiting nervously when Frank arrived at the house, so he'd said a quick hello to Chevis and hustled her into the car. A wool coat covered most of her, so he couldn't tell what she was wearing, but at least it wasn't the navy pea jacket. He'd wanted to take her to the finest restaurant in town, but he'd thought about it and decided he shouldn't come on too strong. For whatever reason—and Frank suspected part of it involved the lawyer in her past—Allie reserved serious involvement for her animals. She just wasn't ready for too romantic a setting... yet.

He glanced over at her. "I do love to see enthusiasm on a date." His head reeled with the scent of clean hair and something else. Something musky—not lemons tonight—something delicately feminine. So she had taken extra pains. Frank felt like shouting his discovery to the world.

She glared at him. "This isn't a date."

"It isn't? What would you call it?" The musky scent was driving him crazy. He opened the window a crack and sucked cold air into his lungs. When he glanced back at her, she was busy twisting a coat button with nervous fingers.

"It's blackmail. So when are you going to tell me what you found out?" She turned her head toward him, her voice soft and husky in spite of her accusation.

"Over dessert." He pulled into the lot of a small steakhouse. Before she could raise further objections, they were sitting at a small table near a stone fireplace. He placed her so that the fire was on her left, the flames reflecting in her lovely green eyes. Frank had called ahead to make sure they got that particular table. "Why don't you take your coat off?"

Allie shrugged off her coat to reveal a white cotton sweater with a sunburst design. The oranges, reds and yellows seemed to touch fire to her hair, bringing new highlights to the already lustrous tumble. "If you don't tell me something, I'm going to explode."

Frank couldn't tell her he was already exploding inside as he gazed at her silhouetted against the setting of stone and dark wood, her hair alive with color. He almost gasped aloud as his eyes devoured her. "You are a very beautiful woman, Allison Tarkington." The dancing flames of the fire brought shadows and a new beauty to her sculptured face.

She squirmed uncomfortably. "Franklin Wade, I didn't come here to hear nonsense like that. I only agreed to come because you said you had information. Now spill." She toyed with a wooden napkin ring, her eyes going again and again to the fire.

Frank's rich laughter filled the cozy alcove by the fireplace. "You're even more beautiful when you're mad." He touched her cheek, gently urging her gaze away from the fire. Firelight danced on dark jade. Frank was sure he could see a longing in her eyes, but perhaps it was a trick of the lighting. "Allie, why can't you accept a compliment?"

"Because you're just saying that." She broke eye contact to watch the waitress put salads in front of them.

His voice was soft and silky. "Oh, but I'm not. It's true. Beautiful and wealthy." He waited for her reaction, although he was not even sure why he'd said it, except that for some reason, he wanted her to know that he knew and that he didn't care. Frank decided not to dwell on the logic of that line of thought in his bemused state.

Allie's fork stopped in mid-air. "Wealthy?" she asked in a weak voice, then gulped. "Where did you hear that?"

"Beautiful wealthy young woman devotes life to animals. Masquerades as flaky commoner. It would make a great book. Why, Allie? Why do you hide with your animals?" His eyes burned into hers as he reached for her hand. "More important than that, why didn't you tell me?"

"Because." Her hand lay unmoving in his as she gazed into the fire, her salad forgotten.

"That's not an answer." Frank knew he was pushing things, but he wanted to know her—who she was, what she was. And if making her a little angry would crack the shell she'd built, then he was willing to risk it.

Allie shifted and looked around the room, then back at Frank. The deep blue in his eyes offered a sanctuary from her pain and isolation. The hunger she had seen moments ago now became a beckoning peace and calm. Suddenly, she wanted him to understand why she did what she did. "Because when you have money, people think you're just another do-gooder interfering in their lives until you get tired of it. Then you're supposed to go on to some other cause. This is not a phase, regardless of what people think—my mother and the powers that be, included." When she realized her fingers were entwined in his, she tensed, then relaxed again, savoring his warmth and strength.

His eyes held hers. "Why couldn't you tell me?"

His eyebrows arched and she knew he needed an answer. But she wasn't even sure why she hadn't told him. She shrugged. "I didn't have a chance to tell you. What was I supposed to do? Sashay into your office and demand you find Dottie, then flutter my eyelashes and say, 'Oh, by the way, I'm wealthy,' as if that should make you look harder?"

Frank smiled. "I guess not, because it wouldn't have made any difference." He wasn't totally happy with that explanation, but he knew it was all he would get right now. "But why animals?" Frank knew that somewhere in the past lay a hurt which Allie had not been willing to forget or forgive. Thus, she had simply withdrawn from the world of men to the safety of animals, whose love was pure and uncomplicated. "Why not hospitals or libraries?" He had to know if all that hurt had to do with men. He had to know if there was some hope that she could love a man again.

"I guess I got my respect for animals from Gran. She was always considered a bit of a rebel when it came to animals and small children. Actually, more of a force to be reckoned with." She smiled at old memories.

"I've always loved animals, but when I was in college, I was at the supermarket one day, and when I came out of my car, there was a kitten there. A starved, ratty little thing that could hardly walk. But he tried to follow me, and when I picked him up he tried to purr." Her eyes misted over at the thought of that moment in her life.

Frank's grip on her hand tightened, his whole being profoundly touched by her glistening eyes. "So you took him home."

She nodded. "Mother had always let us have pets, but they were nice, fat, tidy pets one bought at a pet store. I guess I'd just never thought about the stray ones. Anyway, I started noticing. Next came a dog living in a culvert, then... well, it just happened and here I am with a house and a yard full of beasties." She smiled and shrugged.

Just then, their sizzling steaks arrived. Allie dug into hers, somewhat embarrassed that she'd bared her soul to Frank. She noticed that he was strangely quiet as she concentrated on her steak.

Frank ate his steak, although it might have been a piece of cardboard for all that he tasted of it. He knew there was a big gap somewhere in her story, but he wasn't ready to ask about it. Maybe she did just care that much, but he didn't want it to be that simple. He realized with a start that he wanted her to be running from some awful love affair or something. That would give him more hope. Hell, she wasn't running from anything, she was running *to* something, with a sincerity and caring most people only dreamed of.

And more to the point, why did that bother him so damn much? Probably because he realized in a flash that his plan to satisfy his physical desires for her wasn't good enough for someone like Allie. Which meant... he wrenched his mind away from that line of thought and turned to business. "I found a couple of real questionable things about the lab in Dunbar."

Allie stared at him, confused by his sudden change from very personal to very businesslike. "Like what?" Had there been something in her abbreviated life story that upset him? She'd been close to telling him about the loneliness that attacked her some nights like a hound from hell. She shook off her mood and tried to concentrate on what he was saying.

"Like somebody's trying real hard to keep their interest and ownership in the endeavor under wraps." He was chewing a piece of steak with all the enthusiasm of a dog chewing a stick.

Allie's eyes blinked, then sparkled as the words sank in. "So what do we do now?"

Frank toyed with the wreckage of his steak. "We have not a shred of proof, and, unfortunately, hiding corporate ownership is not against the law."

"Then we'll just have to get the proof. I'll bet there's plenty in that lab." She felt better now that they were discussing crime rather than her.

Frank looked at her sharply. "No. N–O. I've got a few more feelers out." He grinned, seemingly back to his teasing normal self. "We could continue our stakeout—on the mattress."

Allie reddened. "You take the mattress, I'll take the cab." Allie heard the teasing in his voice and relaxed. Teasing was much easier to deal with than silky and serious.

"That does *not* sound like much fun to me," he teased.

"We are not doing this for fun, Frank." She gathered her coat around her as she refused an offer for coffee. All his talk of mattresses was making her uncomfortable. His teasing had a way of becoming silky without warning. Time for a little night air.

"Too bad. Do I have to promise to stay on my side of the mattress?" He rose to help her up.

"They won't come tonight anyway. At least they never have snatched a dog on Wednesday night. Maybe they go to church or something."

Frank froze, his wallet part way out of his pocket, then roared with laughter. "You're kidding."

"Well, how should I know why they skip Wednesdays?" She grinned and started toward the door, leaving Frank to scramble with the bill and then hurry to catch her.

As Frank pulled out into the street, he touched her cheek with his fingers, brushing a strand of hair away from her face. "Sure you don't want to do a little undercover work tonight?" The words teased, but the tone was soft and seductive.

"No. I mean yes, I'm sure." Allie felt even more warm and uncomfortable in the confines of the car. She wondered what he would do if she told him she wanted to ride on the luggage rack. She had sworn after last night that she would never get in a car with him again.

She searched her fevered brain for another reason to end the evening. Obviously Frank didn't think dognappers went to Wednesday night church, and with no stakeout, he might think of some other way for them to spend it. The reality was she couldn't handle another night with him. The darkness hid her flush as she played back the content of her thought. "I have to go by my folks' house tonight and give mother's Cocker her allergy shot."

Frank's eyebrows raised. "You give shots?"

"It's only an allergy shot and Mother and Lisa are too chicken to do it."

"Why don't I run you by there?" Frank wasn't ready for the evening to end. Why should a cocker spaniel get priority?

Allie twisted a lock of hair between her fingers and wondered what she should do. Why hadn't she just told him she had something to do at home? Trading a stakeout for her mother was kind of like going from the frying pan into the fire. She wasn't sure she wanted to let Frank loose around her mother.

If he thought Allie was a little eccentric... maybe he just wanted to find out how well-to-do the family really was. That thought caused a stab of pain deep within Allie—a holdover from another man and another time. She thought that was a disservice to Frank, but then, Bill hadn't seemed interested in money either—at first. "Curious?" Deep down, she knew money had nothing to do with her reluctance to get involved with Frank, but it was a convenient fear to grab hold of.

"Maybe." He shot her an inquisitive look.

"Frank, we're not wealthy, wealthy. We're... well, we're..." Why did she always feel the need to explain away her money—deny her background? After all, that

Cupid's Campaign 97

was what allowed her to do what she wanted to do in life.

He chuckled. "Just plain old wealthy."

"The Vanderbilts are wealthy." She wished the subject had never come up.

"No, they're super wealthy." He squeezed her hand.

"Well, I can't help it."

When he spoke, soft and silky had turned to hard and steel. "You surely don't think that matters to me one way or the other, do you?"

"Well, with some people it does." She might as well get things out in the open right now. She knew now that the only reason she wanted him to see her parents' home was to see his reaction. Then maybe she could convince herself that he was interested in her as a possible campaign resource. That way she wouldn't have to deal with her basic worry—the worry about whether Frank could ever accept her commitment to animals.

The car stopped at a stoplight. Frank turned to her. "Allie, your money or your lack of money is no concern of mine. If I'm curious, it's about your family and knowing a little bit more about you." Surely she didn't think . . .

"Okay, turn right. But I'm not sure you're ready for my mother." Allie suspected that he would take one look at the family and run screaming from the house, and that would be the end of it. Then she wouldn't have to deal with him any more—him and all those warm, fuzzy feelings he caused. Warm, fuzzy feelings that had a way of becoming hot, burning sensations.

"I survived Lisa, didn't I?" He flipped a lock of hair away from her face.

Allie muttered something he didn't catch and directed him to one of the newer parts of town—one of the newer, more elite parts of town. When he had parked the car on a circle drive in front of a very large rambling brick house, he whistled. *"Comfortable?"*

"Well, I can't help it if we have money."

"Allie, dear, I wasn't criticizing it, I was just being impressed." Frank wondered at her sensitivity and had a feeling it was part of the gap in her story at dinner. The more he knew of her, the more complex she became.

"Oh." Allie suspected that none of what she was saying or thinking would make much sense in the harsh light of day.

"My mother would kill for a house like this." He opened her car door.

"Our mothers must have something in common. Mine almost killed Dad worrying him until he bought this one." She opened the door with her own key and hollered into the vast entry hall. An ancient cocker spaniel wobbled toward her, tail wagging. "Hi, Prince." She stopped and ruffled the dog's fur, then led Frank toward the back of the house.

They entered a large den where a middle-aged woman in an expensive jogging suit sat propped up in front of a wide-screen television. "Oh, Allie, dear. How nice to see you. Prince and I wondered where you'd been. His shot was due days ago."

"Mother, Franklin Wade."

From another sofa nearer the television, Lisa's head appeared over the back. "Oh, Allie, how could you? You could at least have called and told us you were coming. I'm a mess." She smoothed her hair and smiled at Frank. "Well, Franklin, this is a surprise."

"Down, girl," Allie growled. "I'll get the stuff out of the refrigerator for Prince." She left and was back in minutes with a syringe.

Jane Tarkington stared openly at Frank. "Well, Allison, I must say this is a definite improvement over the vegetarian."

Frank grinned at Allie who glared up at him from her place near the old dog. "That vegetarian must have been some fellow."

"Perfectly dreadful," Jane replied. "What do you do, Mr. Wade?"

"I'm an assistant prosecutor."

Jane chewed at a fingernail. "Oh, dear. Another lawyer. Well, perhaps this one will work out better."

"Mother," Allie snapped. "He's helping me track down Dottie. And that's all he's doing." She finished giving the shot and rose. "Well, we must be going." She could have kicked Frank for the grin on his face.

Lisa sat up straight. "But I was just going to go make myself presentable."

Allie groaned. "Lisa, we weren't planning to stay all night." She turned to Frank. "It takes her two hours on her face alone. 'Bye everybody." Allie couldn't believe she'd actually convinced herself that bringing Frank here was a good idea. But she wasn't about to prolong the mistake.

Jane rose from her chair. "Allison, one doesn't just run in and run out."

"Mother, I just came by to give Prince his shot." She grabbed Frank's arm.

"Nice to have met you, Mrs. Tarkington." Frank hurried after her.

Allie was silent as Frank headed toward her house. "Allie, what is it? Your mother seems like a very nice person."

"Hmm."

"Allie, I don't understand any of this. One minute

you're worried about me wanting your money, the next you're making excuses because you have that money, and the third you're trying to explain away your mother and sister and their lifestyle." Frank was totally confused by the events of the evening.

"There are more important things in life than tennis and bridge." She huddled into her coat. "And I wasn't worried about you and the money," she said in a low voice.

Frank pulled into her drive and killed the engine, ignoring the din from the backyard. "Allie, look at me." He turned her face toward him with gentle hands, cupping her chin in his hand. "Allie, not everyone cares like you do. Different things are important to different people. You can't expect too much from people. It leads to disappointment." He decided to let the money issue ride and concentrate on her family.

"But they're my family."

"All the more reason not to expect too much. Love is enough in a family." He wanted to understand her pain, to share it.

"Oh, you just don't understand." She dropped her eyes.

"You'd be surprised what I understand. I also understand that I'm rapidly becoming very fond of you." He brushed a kiss on her cheek. "You're a very special person."

Allie sat very still, the warmth wrapping around her like a blanket. "I think I'd better go pill the kitties."

"Allie, you can deny it all you want to, but something happens when we're together. I'd like to pursue it." He brushed a gentle kiss on her lips and felt the now familiar jolt.

Cupid's Campaign 101

"Frank, there is no way you can be attracted to me. We're not . . . we're not . . . anything alike."

Frank somehow sensed that they were finally getting close to her real fear. "Maybe that's it, then." He kissed her gently, the hunger there, but not demanding yet. "Allie, Allie, don't tell me you don't feel that."

"It's physical, it will pass," she said in a small voice.

He pulled her close. "I hope not. Oh, how I hope not." He forced himself to let her go, getting out to open her door. "Allie, it doesn't bother me that we're different." When she didn't respond, he smiled and touched her cheek. "Stakeout tomorrow night, don't forget."

"How could I?" she said breathlessly and fled to the house.

Frank drove slowly, his heart still pounding. What in the hell was he doing? He had virtually forgotten about his campaign, the only work he was doing was on a dognapping case that wasn't even a case, and he couldn't seem to think about anything but Allie.

His physical need for her was almost overwhelming, but he'd come to realize there was more to it than that. He wanted more of her than a few nights in bed. All of which smacked of love. And Frank wasn't ready to fall in love. He faced a long pull before he could commit time and energy to a relationship. And crass as it sounded, Allie was not exactly what he envisioned when he thought of a long term relationship. He'd told her it didn't matter that they were different, and when they were together, it didn't. But Frank knew at some level, deep down, it did bother him. He wasn't even sure why, but it did. Therefore, his feelings must be primarily physical and would, as she'd said, go away.

Frank stalked into his apartment. He must be losing his mind to be thinking about any kind of serious involvement. That kind of thing led to marriage and Frank wasn't interested. Plenty of time for that later. Besides, there was no way she would get involved with someone like him. And he wouldn't get involved with her, so why was he worrying? More to the point, why did he keep trying to convince her they should see more of each other? He told himself that what he was feeling was desire, a sensation that was purely physical. Physical, physical, physical, he repeated to himself as he stepped into the shower.

Chapter Eight

ALLIE HAD SPENT most of the morning trying to figure out a way to tell Frank she didn't want to stake out the neighborhood that night. It wasn't that she didn't want to do it, it was that she didn't want *them* to do it. She'd spent a restless night worrying about the things he'd said to her. Things she wasn't sure she wanted to hear.

Allie had not been passionately in love with the other lawyer, Bill, all those years ago, and they had both been aware of that fact. Everyone had assured her it was a good match and love would come later. Allie had been young and assumed mothers and other people knew better than she about such things, although deep inside she had suffered from serious reservations.

But Bill had been handsome and attentive and ambitious and Allie had begun to fall in love. He'd humored her about all the animals, but she'd sensed he would expect a change after the marriage.

After several months his offering to handle her trust funds had become insistence. Along with his anger at her refusal had come the final realization that Bill was only marrying the name and the money. Allie had hurt long and deep—not so much over a lost love as from disappointment at him for what he was and at herself for being so easily drawn into it. Had he been honest and told her what he wanted, she could have dealt with it, but he had professed love from the first.

All of which had little or nothing to do with Frank. He wasn't like that. But if there was anything Allie knew about, it was herself, and she knew she could not play around with her emotions and feelings. She just felt things too deeply. She knew Frank wanted to make love with her—there was certainly no doubt about that. And Allie would have loved to have a fling with him, but she knew she couldn't just have a fling with Franklin Wade. She was too attracted to him—in ways that surpassed her physical desires. He was the first man she'd met in a long time who felt so strongly about something. She knew he felt about the law the same way she felt about animals rights—no room for compromise. She would get in too deep, then be hurt.

Regardless of Frank's intentions when he was around her, long-term commitment was out of the question. Frank was headed for a great political future, and Allie was simply not cut out to be a politician's wife. She could not compromise her principles for anyone, and her perception of politicians and their wives included a lot of compromise. She was not even sure Frank could handle the compromise, but *he* had to try.

Since Allie could not think of any tactful way to call Frank and tell him she didn't want to meet him at the stakeout that night, she decided she would just play it cool and when he realized she was not interested, he would go away. Hopefully, she could play it cool enough to stay out of trouble but not so cool that he

Cupid's Campaign 105

would go away before they'd found Dottie. Once again, Allie sighed over the fact that relationships with people were so much more complicated than those with animals—particularly those with people who had wonderful blue eyes and made her heart pound and her insides quiver.

Frank stood in his apartment, debating whether to call Allie and tell her something had come up and he couldn't make it tonight. He wanted to see her. No, that wasn't quite accurate. He ached for her, longed to touch her. His control had been exemplary, but he wasn't at all sure he could stand several hours locked in the camper with her. He was afraid he would either force her into something she would regret or make a fool of himself trying. Either way, he was about to explode from pent-up desire.

He put on his coat and looked at the phone one last time. He knew he was getting in too deep, but she had become an obsession with him. He had a bad itch that only Allison Tarkington could scratch. He sighed and walked to his car. He would see her and plead an early morning, then get the hell away from her. It wasn't fair to her or to himself to pursue it.

When Frank tapped on the old camper door and she opened it, all his wonderful plans and logical thoughts flew away like a covey of quail. A tiny battery powered lamp cast soft shadows on her face and turned errant wisps of hair to gold. Frank groaned as all his logical, rational decisions took flight.

Allie leaned out of the camper. "What's wrong? Did you bump your shin or something?"

"You might say I bumped something," he said in a choked voice. *Like my head and scrambled my brains.*

His idea to forget about her suddenly seemed undesirable and impractical.

She stared at him as he stood there sucking in great quantities of cold air. "Are you having a spell of some kind?"

"Umm." He nodded his head rapidly. How could he possibly crawl into that confined space, on that mattress, and make polite conversation? But he couldn't very well stand in the street all night either. Dammit, he was a rational man. He would tell her he had a great physical need for her but couldn't offer anything else. "What I came to tell you—" He caught a whiff of clean hair and lemons.

"Are you going to stay out there?" Allie was clearly puzzled by his actions.

Frank shook his head and crawled over the tailgate, his senses immediately assailed by more lovely lemon scent and kittens. He groaned again.

She laid a hand on his arm. "Are you sure you're all right? Where do you hurt?"

He saw genuine concern in those lovely jade green eyes, flecked gold by the lamplight, and his discomfort grew by leaps and bounds. Why couldn't she just be the flake he'd thought she was? Why did she have to be so damn caring about everything and everyone? He knew she was waiting for an answer and Frank couldn't seem to think of one. He wasn't just about to tell her where he *really* hurt. "Fine. I'm fine. Just a touch of, uh, malaria. Flares up occasionally." *Malaria? You're beginning to sound like a down home version of Humphrey Bogart.*

"Malaria? Frank, when were you in the jungle?" She took her hand off his arm and looked at him suspiciously.

Frank took a deep breath, only to find he'd inhaled a vast amount of lemon and kitten. There was nothing he could do now but brazen it out. "We have very big, very nasty mosquitoes up in Lamar."

Allie giggled. "Frank, there hasn't been a case of malaria in Mississippi since the Civil War."

"How would you know that?"

"Everyone knows that, Frank, except you. Well, maybe there has been, but not around here and not for a long time."

Frank heaved a mighty sigh and laughed. "Well, it was a good try."

"Not very. What is the matter with you tonight?" Allie had scooted away from him as soon as she'd realized he was not in any imminent danger of expiring in the back of her truck.

Determined not to tell her what was really wrong with him, he launched into an explanation of what he'd uncovered that day. As he talked about his investigation, his composure returned. "So the lab is federally licensed, but scuttlebutt has it that they're not always as careful as they should be about bills of sale and proof of ownership."

Allie clapped her hands together. "I knew it. Let's go get 'em, Frank."

"Whoa. We still have to have *something* before we can get a warrant. All I have now is a lot of gossip and speculation." As Frank's mind turned to the legal problem, his heart slowed to a comfortable racing and he stretched out on the mattress facing her, propped up on one elbow.

"Rats. Frank, you're beginning to sound like a broken record. Well, maybe we'll get lucky tonight." She understood Frank's insistence that they follow the letter of the law, but she didn't like it. She looked at his long form stretched lazily across the mattress and swallowed hard. Now that their discussion of business had killed all of three minutes, the long night loomed ahead of them. Frank looked as if he'd settled in for the night.

Allie took a deep breath, determined to tell Frank what she had decided that morning. After all, he *was* helping her, and she owed him honesty. He shifted and she saw long, fine muscles strain against his snug jeans. She would tell him—if she could just remember what it was she'd decided. Tearing her eyes away from his rippling muscles and tight jeans, she thought furiously.

Ah, cool. She would play it cool and he would go away. All she had to do was tell him she couldn't have an affair with him. Somehow it didn't seem as simple as it had in the solitude of her kitchen.

"Frank, I have to talk to you. Seriously."

Frank sprawled out a little more, his back against one side of the camper, his legs even closer to hers. "Talk."

"Well, it's about the other night." She fiddled with the lamp.

"Yes?" His knee touched hers.

"What I mean is, well, I know you feel a certain attraction toward me. I mean I think you do. And—"

He leaned toward her. "I do for a fact." Frank suddenly couldn't seem to remember why he had decided it wasn't fair to pursue a relationship with Allie. It now seemed totally necessary to him to do so.

Allie moved closer to the kittens, so she wouldn't be touching him. "I know this may be presumptuous on my part, but I like to have things understood up front." She coughed and plunged ahead, carefully scrutinizing a bolt on the camper wall. "Anyway, I think I should tell you, I can't well . . . you know."

Cupid's Campaign 109

He leaned even closer and took her hand. His voice was soft. "No, I don't know, Allie. Tell me."

Allie coughed again and tried to retrieve her hand, unable to think with the warmth coursing up her arm. "I guess I'm too intense. I can't just, well, have an affair." There. She'd said it. She quickly continued before she lost her nerve. "And that doesn't mean I'm looking for any commitment from you. After all, we hardly know each other. But if you were thinking of something long term, well, it wouldn't work anyway, because I would be a liability to your political future and if I got too involved with you, then I wouldn't want to let you go, and then one or both of us would be hurt, and if we have a clear understanding before any of this happens, then we can find Dottie and be friends and no one will get hurt." She paused, breathless from what she knew must be the longest sentence in the history of the English language. "Uh, could I have my hand back, please?"

Frank's deep chuckle filled the camper. "I've heard of people who spoke in paragraphs, but I never knew one." Then his laughter was gone, his face serious as he took her face in his hands and kissed her. "Oh, Allie, my honest, straightforward little Allie. Do you really think it was my rational, logical legal mind which brought me here tonight?" He tapped his chest. "It's what I feel in here that brought me. And neither you nor I have any control over what we feel in here. It started the first day I saw you." All Frank's doubts and reservations fled into the night.

Allie gazed into his eyes, deep and blue as a tropical sea in the lamplight, burning with a hunger she felt in her deepest being. "But it's physical. And I'm trying to tell you—"

He placed gentle fingers on her lips. "A part of it is physical, no question, but when I'm with you, I feel something I've never felt before, Allie. Maybe it's love, maybe not, but we owe it to ourselves to follow it where it may lead, not cut it off before we have a chance to find out." His fingers traced the outline of her lips.

"But that's what I'm trying to tell you," she wailed. "It can't possibly lead anywhere."

"I can't accept that, honey. Don't you think I've struggled with my feelings? I spent half the afternoon thinking of all the reasons I shouldn't be here tonight— all the reasons why we shouldn't see each other. But here I am. Give it a chance, Allie." Before she could respond, his mouth descended on hers, his kiss gentle yet not disguising his deep longing. Then he leaned back, still holding her hands in his. "I won't push you, but I won't go away either. Not until I know what might be."

Somewhere in the recesses of Allie's mind, the flame of love flickered to life, fed by hope and trust. Allie's hope of finding a man who could love her for what she was had lain dormant for so long. Trust had been a fleeting thing, cast back in her face, now offered again by Frank. Her heart soared, her reservations forgotten in the moment. She returned his kiss with a new ardor.

"You will give it a chance, won't you, Allie?" He held her face in his hands.

As she answered him with a kiss, she became aware of scratching sounds on the back of the camper. She stared at Frank, unable to shake off the effects of his kisses. "Who could that be?" she whispered.

"It's your camper," he whispered back and reached to open the door. He just hoped Ken hadn't come calling again.

For a moment, they couldn't see anyone, then a somewhat familiar face appeared from the side of the truck. Allie finally realized it was her grandmother with something black smeared on her face. "Gran, what are you doing here?"

Elspeth signaled to someone and Triola and Gladys appeared from behind a large oak tree, Gladys carrying a picnic basket, Triola a Thermos. "It's nippy tonight, Allison. We thought you might need sustenance. We haven't blown your cover, have we?" Elspeth's whisper could have been heard clear to the next block.

Allie felt Frank rumbling with muffled laughter beside her. "That's very thoughtful, Gran, but you shouldn't have." As Allie leaned over the tailgate, it came crashing down. "Damn. Of all the times for this stupid thing to decide to work." She slapped the tailgate with a resounding blow.

"Oh, I'm so glad it's finally working, Allison. We can spread things out right here. Young man, bring the lamp."

As Frank handed the lamp to Elspeth and watched, the ladies spread all manner of sandwiches and cookies on the tailgate, he whispered to Allie. "I sincerely hope Ken doesn't show up tonight." China cups and saucers appeared from the depths of the basket.

Allie ran a finger over Elspeth's blackened face. "Gran, where on earth did you find whatever is on your face?"

"The cellar, my dear. We used to burn coal and there is still some dust in the corners. Does it make me invisible?" she asked eagerly.

"You're just a fleeting shadow in the night, Gran," Allie assured her.

Triola spoke in a loud whisper. "I've had pains in my

knee all day, Allison. I just know those men will come tonight."

Gladys rolled her eyes toward the heavens. "Triola, that means it's going to rain."

Triola harumphed loudly. "It isn't a rain pain, Gladys. It's different."

Elspeth arranged everything to her satisfaction and turned to the ladies. "Off we go, girls. We don't want anything to appear out of the ordinary tonight on the Avenue." With that, the trio started back toward Elspeth's.

As soon as the ladies' whispers about rain pains versus omen pains faded to a respectable distance, Allie and Frank collapsed into each other's arms, laughing so hard they almost upset the carefully laid out tea party. Frank finally wiped his tears of laughter from his eyes and took a sandwich. "Of course, they don't think a tailgate party in the middle of the night is out of the ordinary."

"Of course not." Allie took a cookie and poured coffee for them. "Nothing like a catered stakeout, I always say." She took a bite of cookie and shook her head. "Bless their hearts. You know, when that generation of ladies is gone, their kind won't pass this way again."

Frank nodded as he heard the love and emotion in her voice. "Your grandmother is handling this very well."

"That generation was taught to handle all things well."

They had turned to serious eating in a companionable silence when headlights turned the corner down the block. Afraid Ken might come calling again, they both dived into the camper and Allie quickly threw an old towel over the tea party.

A truck lumbered by and the driver cut the lights as

soon as it had started down Jefferson. It slowed and stopped some twenty yards ahead of them. Suddenly they heard the muffled barking of dogs. "Frank, it's them," Allie whispered, clutching his arm.

"The camera. Where's the camera?"

Allie thrust the infrared camera into his hands and started digging in her jacket pockets. "Damn, I can't find the car keys." She had flipped off the lamp when they heard the truck. She felt around the mattress.

Frank slipped out of the truck and stood behind the oak tree, shooting pictures of the truck while Allie dug around for her keys. The other truck started up and pulled away. Frank ran back to the truck. "We have to follow them."

"I can't find the damn... here they are." She leapt out of the truck, then stopped and started shoving things into the camper.

"Come on, we'll lose them."

"I'll lose my head if I leave Gran's china in rubble on the street."

"She won't care. Hurry up."

"But I'll care." Then she was in the cab cranking the old truck. When they got to the end of Jefferson, the truck was nowhere in sight. Allie drove through the neighborhood, hoping to spot them again, fuming that they had blown probably the only chance they would have. "How could they have just disappeared? We weren't that far behind them."

Frank's voice held no humor. "They've probably got more horses under that hood than a police cruiser. But we got the license number on film. We can trace them easily enough," Frank said reassuringly.

"What if it's a stolen tag or something?" Allie couldn't believe they'd been so busy eating and drinking and... other things that they'd missed the damn thieves.

"Don't borrow trouble. Where can we get these developed?" He started to suggest they drive to Dunbar and wait for the truck, but decided that was too dangerous for Allie. They'd pulled it off once, but those men might not ignore them a second time.

"I can do it." She headed for home.

"You? Don't tell me you have the equipment to develop infrared."

"It doesn't take special equipment. I can do it on mine." She heard his incredulous mutterings. "Well, otherwise you have to send film away and it takes forever. I never have forever."

Silence reigned as they drove back to Allie's, each consumed with private thoughts. When they arrived, Allie carried the kittens, Frank the camera. He knew she was flogging herself mentally for missing the opportunity to follow the thieves—if the truck had indeed held the thieves. He also realized how very important this was to Allie. He hoped it wasn't a stolen tag or truck, but he knew that was a strong likelihood.

Chevis greeted them as if they'd been gone for a lifetime and it was several minutes before he calmed down. Allie put the kittens in their bed and led Frank down steep steps to a basement. Chevis stood at the door and howled when they refused to let him go.

A part of the basement had been walled off and Frank followed her into a fully equipped darkroom. He watched, fascinated, as Allie quickly and efficiently prepared the film tank. She flipped off the light and the darkness was total. "This darkroom is incredible, Allie," Frank said, feeling disoriented in the blackness.

"It is nice, isn't it? It's taken me a long time to get

Cupid's Campaign 115

everything I need. Of course, I had to take hours of courses to learn how to use it all, not to mention the photography courses."

Frank sensed her presence close to him, the scent of her hair and clothing accentuated by his inability to see her. He started to reach for her, then stopped, although he knew he could unerringly find her. "You no doubt started taking pictures of animals very early in life." His voice sounded loud to him.

"How did you know?"

"Just a wild guess." He heard her move and assumed she had leaned against the old desk where the enlarger sat. He didn't know if it was the darkness or something else, but her voice sounded strained.

"Umm. My mother used to ration out the film. I'd take thirty-six pictures of a sleeping dog. Thirty-six identical pictures. She wasn't crazy about that." Allie touched something on the wall and an eerie red light flooded the room.

Frank chuckled and saw that the red light made her hair glow with fire. He glanced around the room and noticed animal pictures. Others were strewn on every available flat surface. He picked up a picture. The dog's face and length were that of a Dachshund, the color and size were not. "Is this Dottie?"

She glanced at the picture and nodded, busy with chemicals and the reel she had removed from the tank. "It has to dry now."

"So what do you take pictures of now?"

"Everything. But mostly, pictures of animal abuse for evidence. That's why it's important for the equipment to be top notch. Some of my stuff is in that file cabinet." She motioned to a four drawer file in the corner and turned back to the film.

Frank wandered over to it, anxious to see some of her work. He pulled open the top drawer and took out a handful of glossy eight-by-tens, expecting to see some of her sleeping dogs. He was not ready for what he saw—starvation, brutality, man's inhumanity to his fellow creatures. His stomach knotted. "My God, Allie, how do you stand it?"

"I just have to take the pictures, Frank. The question is, how do they stand it?" She turned to look at him, her skin fiery red in the strange light.

Frank crossed the distance and gathered her in his arms. "Oh, Allie, my poor, sweet Allie. And you carry all that with you every day."

She nodded against his chest. Her arms tentatively circled his waist. Then she was clinging to him, hot tears flowing.

Frank held her and stroked her back. He knew she had never shared those pictures or her pain with anyone and he felt something touch his very soul that she would trust him with both. A need to hold her and protect her forever swept over him. When he felt the shuddering sobs quiet, he tilted her face up to his and gently kissed her eyelids. The kisses held not physical desire but fierce protectiveness and a sharing he'd never felt before. Love settled on Frank like a warm blanket.

Allie wiped her face and sniffled. "I'm sorry. I don't know why I did that."

He kissed her again. His voice trembled with emotion. "You can't carry the whole world on your shoulders alone, Allie."

"I know, but I can try." She smiled, trying to hide the trembling in her lower lip.

"I can help you carry it, honey." He wiped her tears with gentle fingers.

"It gets awfully heavy sometimes, Frank."

"But I have very strong shoulders."

She looked at him for a long moment and started to say something. But then she turned away. "I think the negatives are ready."

Frank knew she had retreated back into her protective shell, a shell he was now determined to crack, releasing the delicate flower within. At that moment, he knew he was hopelessly in love with this lovely creature who could face the brutality he'd seen in those pictures and not become embittered, just keep calmly hacking away at the problem.

She quickly placed the negatives in the enlarger and exposed them on paper, then transferred them to a tray of chemical. As the pictures began to take form on the paper, she leaned close. "Not bad."

"I used to take pictures of rocks. I'll bet they'd go well with your sleeping dogs." He looked over her shoulder at the eerie pictures of a truck with a license plate clearly visible. For that matter, the truck should be easily identified. One angle shot showed a deep crease which started at the right front fender and went straight back to the rear of the truck.

Allie washed and fixed the prints, then hung them to dry. As they waited in uneasy silence, Frank wanted to sweep her up and carry her away from the pictures he had seen, away from her pain and suffering, keep her safe. Even as he thought it, he knew it was not what she wanted. She wanted to make a difference in a world which, at times, seemed beyond caring. He knew her silence was because of what had passed between them. She busied herself with things which did not need doing.

When the prints were finally dry, Frank took one of

them off the line. "I'll run the license first thing in the morning." He lingered, waiting for some sign that she would be all right, that she would maybe share her feelings with him, but she didn't turn to him.

"You'll let me know?" Her voice held such sadness.

He stepped behind her and brushed a kiss on her cheek. "As soon as I know." He slipped out of the darkroom and up the stairs, sensing that Allie wanted to be alone, didn't want to say good-bye to him in the harsh lights of the kitchen. He didn't want to leave her like that, but he knew it was what she wanted.

As Frank drove home, a cold rage began to grow. It was the same rage he felt when a kid died from drugs. It was a rage at the injustices of the world. And Frank knew, just as sure as the sun would come up in the morning that he would catch the men who had stolen Dottie. It might not be in time to save her, but it would be in time to save others from what he'd seen in some of those pictures which had obviously been taken in research facilities that used the Dotties they stole.

As Frank walked to his front door, he not only looked like a Viking warrior, he felt like one.

Chapter Nine

FRANK SAT AT his desk studying the information he had neatly outlined on a yellow legal pad. Ken Villines had called him earlier with the license number trace. The vehicle, an eighty-four Chevy pickup, was registered to Lonnie Dykes. The same Lonnie Dykes, Frank assumed, who was listed on one of the many corporations involved in the Dunbar lab. The same Lonnie Dykes who just happened to be Max's brother-in-law, a man Frank had met once or twice when he came to the office to see Max. Frank tried to remember what he was like, but the only memory that would come was that of a sullen man dressed in polyester.

Frank was ready to go for a warrant on Mr. Dykes, even though he didn't have quite as much probable cause as he needed. What stopped him was the fact that theoretically, Max should sign the warrant. Frank doodled on the pad. The big question was whether or not Max was involved in the whole thing.

What he needed right now was Allie. He needed to talk things through with someone, even though he knew

Allie would opt for the warrant. He picked up the phone, thinking an early lunch with her might help him decide.

Allie sat at her kitchen table watching Chevis and the kittens play—or rather watching the kittens clamber around on the dog as if he were a mountain of some sort. Ordinarily, the antics would have made her laugh, but this morning, only a faint smile played at her mouth. A cup of lukewarm coffee sat on the table.

What to do about Franklin Wade, the prosecutor who cared. After last night, there was no longer any doubt that he cared, or that she cared. Allie had never broken down like that in front of anyone—much less a man, certainly not a lawyer. And Allie had come to the startling realization that here was a man with whom she might like to share her life—a man with whom she *could* share her life. Of course, it was much too soon to think about love and marriage and such, but it was time to think about exploring the possibility of those possibilities.

Allie took a drink of cold coffee and made a face. Frank had made it pretty clear he didn't care about her eccentricities, but Allie was a realist. Somehow, she had to show him that she was perfectly capable of adapting to whatever situation might arise—that she could change into the kind of woman Allie was sure Frank wanted and needed.

He would never say anything, but there was little doubt in Allie's mind that he had considered the problem of taking her campaigning in her faded jeans and surplus jacket. No, if she were going to think about a relationship with Frank, she had to prove to him that she would be an acceptable mate for a politician—in the

Cupid's Campaign 121

unlikely event things ever went that far. Allie had thought long and hard about whether or not she was willing to make significant changes in her life. She still wasn't sure she was, but she knew she had to give it serious consideration if she wanted Frank. And she wanted Frank—for however long he would have her.

In the meantime, it was Friday, and Dottie would be shipped out Sunday night or early Monday morning. Allie had already made her decision about that problem—a decision which did not include Frank. In fact, she would have to figure out some way to get rid of him over the weekend.

The phone rang, and Allie brightened considerably at the sound of Frank's voice. He sounded down, and she felt a knot of fear curdle her morning coffee. "What is it, Frank?"

"Hey, don't worry, I have some good news." His voice denoted anything but good news.

"So why do you sound like you're going to a funeral?"

"Well, good news always goes hand in hand with bad news, doesn't it?" There was a long pause. "Allie, can you meet me for lunch? I need to talk to you about this one."

Allie's fear reached icy fingers toward her heart. Had he found Dottie . . . dead? "Frank—"

"As soon as you can make it, Allie. Sunshine Coffee Shop."

As Allie hurried toward the door, the phone rang again. It was Gran.

"Allison, you must come right away."

"Gran, what is it?"

"Allison, we've been out in the neighborhood this

morning and we've found a clue. No, clues are in mystery books. We've found evidence."

"What, Gran?" Allie had to talk to Frank before she could see Elspeth. She had to know if he'd found... something.

"Bring your young man and come as soon as you can, dear."

Allie's mind raced. "Uh, he may be busy, but we'll be there as soon as we can, Gran." Allie didn't know how she would face her grandmother if she had to be the one to tell her that Dottie was... gone. She fought back tears which threatened to well up as she started the old truck.

Frank was waiting in the small coffee shop near the courthouse when Allie arrived. He brushed a kiss on her cheek as he seated her. "Hi."

"Hi." Allie fiddled with her glass of water. "Gran called. She and the ladies allegedly have a clue—a piece of real evidence, even. Can we run by there after lunch?" She tried to keep her voice bright as she looked at the frown on Frank's handsome face.

"Sure." He looked across the table. "Allie—"

"Frank, is Dottie... is she—"

He quickly took her hands. "No. I mean, I don't know." He watched her eyes mist over. "Oh, Allie, I'm sorry. Did you think I wanted to tell you that I'd found her?"

She nodded.

"Oh, honey. Damn, I should have known that's what you'd think. I'm sorry." He took a deep breath. "No, this is about the license number." After they'd ordered, he quickly explained what he'd found.

Allie stared at him, relief about Dottie clearly written on her face. "So what are we doing sitting here?"

He laid a hand on hers. "It's not as simple as it sounds. I can do one of two things. Just prepare the arrest warrant and full steam ahead, or I can go to Max and let him try to explain. At least give him some time to prepare himself."

Allie snorted. "You mean time to warn his brother-in-law so they can skip."

"And what if Max is not involved? What if he has no idea what Lonnie is doing? That would make me a real heel."

"How can he not know?" Allie was becoming impatient with all the rhetoric.

"Do you know everything your family is involved in?" Dammit, he wanted her to understand, not just assume Max was a crook.

"No, but I'd know if it were illegal."

"I doubt that. In fact, that's the last thing you'd know. It would be a cruel thing for me to issue a warrant for Lonnie behind Max's back. Not even give him a hint. I just can't do it." He could see the defiance and anger in her eyes, for all that she wasn't expressing it.

"I thought you didn't like him." Allie swirled her glass, watching the tiny whirlpool, listening to the ice cubes tinkle against the sides. On an intellectual level, she understood Frank's dilemma, but right now she wasn't interested in the intellectual side of the issue.

Frank shrugged. "I don't particularly like him as a person, but I respect him and he brought me into the office. He's let me handle a lot of things because he trusts me."

Allie looked at the sandwich which had appeared before her. "Frank, what if he is involved and squeals? You know what will happen to the dogs in that lab?"

Frank nodded and pushed his meal away, untouched. His eyes reflected his warring emotions. "You think I haven't thought of that? Do you also think I haven't thought of what will happen if I go ahead and we find absolutely nothing at that lab or in Lonnie's possession? That's the problem when you only have weak probable cause instead of evidence."

Allie wanted to understand, wanted to sympathize with Frank's dilemma, but mostly she wanted to go break up that lab and Lonnie Dykes. She squeezed his hand in sympathy, but inside she boiled with anger. "So what are you going to do?" She would not try to influence him, much as she wanted to. It might backfire.

He finally smiled. "Let's go see what your grandmother has. Maybe they have a footprint in a flowerbed or something."

Allie laughed. "It's more likely they have some poor unsuspecting delivery man locked in the pantry."

The trip to Elspeth's passed in virtual silence, both busy with their own thoughts. Allie had already decided that if Frank didn't do something by Sunday night, she would go to the lab and do what she had to do. That decision made, she was free to worry about what she was going to do about Frank. A germ of a plan had started to grow.

Elspeth, Gladys and Triola were anxiously waiting in the carport when they drove in. They were on Allie in a minute, all talking at once.

"Well, I found it," Gladys crowed.

"But it was my idea," Triola chimed indignantly.

"It may well have been, but it was hardly where you thought it might be," Gladys retorted.

Cupid's Campaign

In spite of their somber mood, Frank and Allie smiled at each other, trying to figure out what the ladies were talking about. As the heated discussion continued, laughter replaced the smiles. It was impossible to break into the conversation.

Elspeth stepped up. "Girls, please. What is important is the evidence." She produced a little red collar, studded with rhinestones. "Gladys found this in the next block. We did a little investigation on our own this morning at Triola's suggestion." Elspeth smiled at the group.

Frank noted that Gladys and Triola seemed happy now that they had been awarded their proper credit. He turned the collar over in his hand his face void of all laughter. "Who did it come off of?"

"Greywolf," the ladies chimed together.

Frank stared at the collar. "Greywolf? Is that a real—"

Allie took the collar. "Not a wolf, not even close."

"It's from Mildred Grimley's Schnauzer. Mildred thought he looked like a little wolf when he was a puppy. He disappeared last night."

Allie gave Frank a questioning look. "Isn't that enough?"

Frank looked from the eager faces back to the little collar, his anger growing as he realized what the little dog must have suffered last night, its struggles enough to wrench the collar off. "I'll do what I can," he said harshly.

Allie bubbled as they drove back to her truck. "Surely we can do something now, Frank."

Frank concentrated on his driving, knowing there was damn little he could do legally with one red collar found on the street. Since no one had seen the dog kidnapped, or even seen the truck in the vicinity of the dog, it represented little. They might know or strongly suspect what had happened, but it lent very little to building a tight case against Lonnie Dykes. "It's not much, Allie. The dog could still be in the neighborhood."

"You know better than that."

"What I know or suspect is not enough, Allie." He felt her tense beside him. "Look, I'll do what I can. Which means, I'll keep digging." He pulled into a parking place beside her truck.

"Will you warn Max?"

"I don't know yet. I'll let you know."

Allie was halfway out of the car when she remembered her plan and turned back to him. "Oh, I wondered if you'd be interested in having dinner at my place tonight?"

As Frank looked up into her dazzling smile, Dottie and Greywolf and everything else was forgotten as his brain seemed to stop functioning in favor of his heart. He reached for her hand. "I'd like that very much."

"See you at seven."

Frank drove back to his office in a daze. He'd fully expected Allie to be enraged by his failure to rush out and have Lonnie arrested. Instead, she'd invited him to dinner. His heart sang. She had finally realized, rather admitted to herself, that she felt something for him, and that they should pursue it.

When Frank stepped into the office, however, his elation dimmed as he walked toward Max's office. Somewhere during the morning, he had made the decision to confront Max with his information. He owed Max that much. Taking a deep breath, he turned toward Max's office. "Max in?" he asked the secretary.

She shook her head. "Out for the afternoon. It's Friday, remember?" Max had a habit of taking off a Friday now and then.

Frank slammed into his office. He'd made up his mind, now he wanted to get it over with. He sat down to prepare the arrest warrant.

Chapter Ten

ALLIE LOOKED AROUND the house nervously. She had spent most of the day cleaning and preparing for dinner. As she fluffed her hair in the mirror one last time, she thought how ridiculous the whole thing was. Dottie was near the end of her time and Allie was busy trying to convince a man that she was suitable for civilized company.

Of course, Allie had spent most of the day rationalizing her strange behavior. She would take care of Dottie regardless of what Frank decided to do. But once the business with Dottie was over, then her daily contact with Frank would be at an end. And, in her mind, that meant he would go back to his campaign and his prosecuting—and probably realize that she had been an interesting diversion, but certainly not someone who could fit into his life on any long term basis.

Allie had decided she had to prove differently to him before he had time to come to that conclusion. Oh, he had talked about relationships and such, but she was sure that was just in the heat of the moment—the grip of passion rather than the throes of love. She gazed around the cozy house. Well, she would prove to Franklin Wade that she could be as elegant and civilized and ... whatever else it was she thought he might want in a woman.

What time she hadn't been worrying about her behavior, she'd spent worrying about what would happen if Frank told Max about the arrest warrant. She hoped he hadn't, because one of her goals for the evening was to convince him not to tell Max.

Allie smoothed the silk dress. She knew she looked nice, although she would have felt much better in jeans. She certainly had no plans to seduce Frank, but maybe she could use her wiles to keep him from going to Max. That is if she could remember how one went about using one's wiles. It had never been one of her stronger points. She brushed at a speck of dust on the gleaming walnut table and had started to rearrange the silver when the doorbell rang.

Frank gasped when she opened the door, unable to do anything but stand and stare. A vision of loveliness stood before him. A simple silk dress the color of old ivory clung to her slender curves. A filmy silk scarf followed the neckline, the greens in the scarf picking up and accentuating the greens in her eyes. The simple lines of the dress were unbroken except for the scarf and a brooch. Silky hose covered her legs and as Frank's eyes trailed steadily down from her face, he realized he'd never really seen her legs before. They were as perfect as he'd known they would be.

"Uh, you are coming in, aren't you?" She took a step closer to him, wondering if he was in shock or if he didn't recognize her. Maybe he thought he'd wandered into the wrong house.

"Oh, sorry. Yes." Frank felt as flustered as a teenager on a first date as he followed her down the hall, clutching a bottle of wine in a death grip. Her hair floated in front of him, brushed to a fiery sheen. He couldn't believe he'd come to the right house, and he couldn't imagine why she'd gone to so much trouble, but he loved it.

When he stepped into the kitchen, delicious aromas assailed him. The clutter had disappeared and the room glowed in the soft light of lamps. "What's the occasion?" His eyes devoured her.

Allie shrugged and flashed him a dazzling smile. "Oh, I just thought you might like something besides a microwave special tonight. Wine?"

She handed him a corkscrew and for a moment, he couldn't imagine why. All he could do was stand and stare. When she waved toward the forgotten bottle in his hand, he smiled. "Oh. Right." He quickly uncorked the bottle and handed it to her. There was no way he would be able to manage crystal glasses with his whole body running away with itself.

He accepted a glass of the white wine, closing his fingers carefully around the delicate crystal. His eyes caught sight of the walnut table in the living room, picture perfect with its twinkling crystal, polished silver and patterned placemats and napkins. He shook himself, unable to believe the change in the house since he'd been there last. Or the changes in the mistress of the house. Scented candles twinkled throughout the living room, making his head swim. "You didn't have to go to so much trouble, you know." He stood close to her, not touching, but close enough to catch her musky smell. He reached up and touched her hair.

"Oh, it wasn't any trouble." She took one long look into his eyes and busied herself at the stove.

Frank smiled and sipped the wine. His shock began to fade as the strangeness of the whole setting began to soak in. Then knowledge of what she was doing began to dawn. She'd done it all for him. He still wasn't sure why, but he suspected... surely not. She wasn't the type to try and seduce anyone. Not that he would resist.

"Allie, I live alone, remember? I know all about marathon cleaning when you expect company." He stepped closer until his body touched the silk of her back. A shock passed between them and he heard her soft intake of breath. "I thought maybe I'd gone beyond the company stage," he murmured into her ear.

"Well, I did do a little cleaning." She ducked away from him to tend a steaming pan.

Frank stepped back and walked around the kitchen, knowing if he didn't, they would never make it to dinner. A mournful howl came from the back of the house. "Where's Chev?" Frank scanned the room. Not an animal in sight.

"Out back." She carefully arranged vegetables on a serving platter.

"Why?" No wonder the house had seemed strange. He'd gotten used to all the cats and the big Shepherd.

Allie transferred the platter to the table. "Well, Chev is hardly conducive to a... well, to—"

His eyes burned into hers, holding her motionless. "To what, Allie?" He crossed the distance between them, his eyes never leaving hers. "To a quiet, romantic dinner?"

She swallowed hard, afraid her voice had abandoned her. "He sometimes gets carried away with his enthusiasm. The table and all." She knew she wasn't making sense, but the only sense in her world right now was the desire in those burning blue eyes.

"It's okay, Allie. I like Chev." He stroked her cheek with the back of his fingers. And suddenly he knew why the big dog had been confined to the backyard. He knew why she had worked so hard. Allie was trying to show him that she could be what she thought he needed. He sighed deep within himself. Hadn't he made it clear to her it didn't matter? Frank's love for her grew as the realization of her effort grew, and he couldn't think of any way to tell her he didn't want her to change—any way that wouldn't embarrass her or hurt her feelings.

"Maybe after dinner," she murmured as another howl shattered the night. "Blast." She dished up chicken and hurried to the dining table.

Frank smiled at her lapse into the Allie he loved, but followed her to the table, determined to give her the evening of elegance. He seated her and bent close, his lips touching her throat. "This is beautiful, Allie, and so are you." He felt her shiver and sat down across from her, the room lit only by the shimmering aquariums and a single candle on the table.

Allie gazed at him across the table, his eyes flickering in the candlelight, and forgot her beautifully prepared dinner. Nothing seemed to exist except the man—the man with whom she was falling hopelessly in love. Warmth enveloped her, warmth and a longing the likes of which she had never felt. As his hand covered hers, she thought she would ignite right where she sat. The pressure of his hand jogged her slightly and Allie knew she would never get through dinner if she didn't distract herself. "What did you do about Max?" she asked in a soft, husky voice.

Frank was not about to let business interfere with his

Cupid's Campaign 133

reeling senses. "After dinner." He loosed her hand and sipped wine, although the wine couldn't begin to match the intoxication he already felt. His desire for her became a living, raging need, far beyond any sexual desire he had ever experienced. He wanted her—all of her. With a force of will, he began to eat the lovely meal, for to not eat would be a disservice to her hard work.

"It's a delicious dinner," he said in a velvety voice, going through the motions of eating, yet hardly taking his eyes off her. She was a vision of loveliness in the elegant setting, but Frank knew deep down it was not the setting in which his Allie belonged. She belonged in her jeans and funny hat, a puppy or kitten cradled to her breast. And that was how Frank would take her. It was who she was. To take that away from her would be to take away her heart and soul. She could move with grace in any world, but her world of animals and caring was what made her unique and . . . it was who he loved. He searched for the words.

"I hoped you would like it." Her words were as stilted and out of place as her dress—not Allie. She cleared the dinner things and set a piece of cake before him.

Frank felt a surge of relief when the meal ended and she poured coffee and brought brandy snifters. He wanted to hold her, tell her he loved her just the way she was, not the way she thought he wanted her to be. As she poured brandy, Chevis's pitiful howl came again, this time a cry of absolute and total desolation. He stayed her hand with a gentle touch, his eyes seeking hers. "Allie, let him in. He'll get a complex or something."

Allie sighed and went to the back door. Chevis bounded in, his feet tangled in the four cats scrambling to come in too. Chevis greeted them as if he'd been marooned for years. But the cats slowed to a walk and strolled toward the living room, casting indignant looks at Allie. Allie fussed as Chevis continued to whine and bounce around the room. "Now if you're going to be in here, try to act civilized." She finally shamed the big dog into lying down in the living room at her feet. The liquid brown eyes gazed at his mistress as if she had beaten him within an inch of his life.

Frank pulled Allie close to him as he dropped to the sofa. "It was a beautiful dinner, Allie. Thank you."

She smiled and sipped the brandy. "I haven't done that in a long time." She gently removed the cat who had materialized on her lap and ignored the one on the table licking a cake plate by candlelight.

His fingers toyed with the nape of her neck, and he smiled as he felt the quivers run through her body. "You're very good at it."

"Out of practice." She nudged Chevis with her foot as he inched closer to her and began sniffing her shoes.

Frank sensed that she was somewhat tense and not totally comfortable and wondered how to ease her situation. He wanted to tell her to go change into jeans or her sweatsuit and come back to him, bubbling and feisty and full of life. "Do you think you need to get back into practice?"

She shrugged. "One never knows, does one?" Chevis had now worked his way up to her hose and was applying his huge nose like a vacuum cleaner. "Chev, go. Otherwise, you're going to end up back outside." The dog gave her a mournful look and stopped for approximately two seconds, then continued. A cat crept down the back of the sofa toward her lap.

Frank couldn't imagine what the dog was doing, but

whatever it was, it was making Allie very tense and edgy. The behavior of the animals clearly indicated they thought their mistress was behaving very oddly. Frank wanted to laugh at their antics, but knew that would be a terrible mistake. "Well, I kind of liked you in sweat pants," he murmured as he pulled her closer, nuzzling her neck. His hand touched the brooch. "That's very old, isn't it?"

She nodded, glaring at a third cat who was now flanking her from the lamp table. "It's Gran's. Grandad gave it to her when they were married." She looked down at the brooch, all burnished gold and filigree with a tiny painting in the center.

"It's almost as lovely as the one who wears it."

She gave him a strange look and pushed at Chevis, who by now had started his vacuum cleaner routine on her silk dress. "Dammit, Chev, get lost," she said in a tightly controlled voice.

Frank couldn't contain his curiosity a minute longer. "What is he doing? Do you have dog cookies hidden or something?"

"He's being rude." At that moment, the two cats landed on Allie, one skidding down her front from a miscalculated jump, the other leaping from the sofa back into her lap. Chevis landed in the middle of all of them, panting happily. Allie threw them off as she jumped up. "Well, hell, I should have known I'd never be able to pull it off—not with all this help." She glared at the animals, her face flushed.

Frank stood quickly and took her trembling hands. "Allie, it's okay. Believe me, it's okay." He took her in his arms.

She turned misty eyes up to him. "Oh, Frank, I wanted things to be perfect."

"They are perfect, honey." He stroked her hair and brushed gentle kisses on her face.

"No, they're not. They're a mess. I should have known I couldn't bring it off. I just should have known, then I wouldn't have tried."

He tilted her chin up, concern etching his face. He thought he knew what she'd tried, but he wanted her to say it. "Allie, what are you talking about?"

Her lower lip trembled. "All this." She waved toward the animals. "You know what the big dummy's doing?" Chevis grinned happily as his nose worked up the back of her dress.

"I haven't the first clue," Frank replied, although he was pretty sure he knew exactly what the dog's problem was.

"This dress has hung in the closet so long, he's never even seen me in it. These clothes are strange to him."

Before Frank could stop himself, he laughed. Of course, the dog would give her away, and Allie of all people should know that. He felt Allie tense and knew he'd blown it. He kissed her gently, but the tension increased. "Honey, Chev is right. You are a stranger in those clothes. A very lovely stranger, but a stranger nonetheless."

She turned away from him. "You don't have to make fun of me. I was trying."

He gathered her in his arms. "Sweetheart, I'm not making fun of you, but Chev and I feel the same. I just didn't have the nerve to be quite so blatant about it." He stood back and looked into her eyes. "Allie, I didn't fall in love with a woman in silk, I fell in love with a woman who cared too much about two little kittens to let them die. I didn't lose my heart to crystal and gour-

Cupid's Campaign 137

met dinners, I lost my heart to spaghetti in the kitchen while you fed and nurtured those kittens."

Her eyes glistened and one big tear ran down her cheek. "But you can't. You need someone else. The governor's wife doesn't take in stray kittens."

He kissed her cheek dry. "Then the governor should get a new wife." Frank started to kiss her, then grinned. "Did I hear you say wife?"

Her cheeks reddened. "No. I mean yes, but I didn't mean it. It was just an example."

"I kinda like the idea."

She twisted away from him and stood up. "No, Frank. You're getting distracted. You may find this situation amusing now, but you wouldn't the first time you were embarrassed by me. What would you do when Chevis stuck his nose up the vice-president's wife's dress? Think about that."

"Surely Chev has better taste than that."

Allie stomped the floor with a daintily shod foot. "You're not taking this seriously, Frank." Chevis lay down and began licking one of Allie's shoes, his eyes glazed with happiness.

Frank stood and towered over her. "Dammit, you could never embarrass me. And Chev goosing the vice-president's wife would make great copy. Chev is right and seemingly smarter than his mistress tonight. You shouldn't change for me or anyone else."

"Then there's no future for us. I can change, you know. Dammit, Chev, I'm going to punch your lights out if you don't stop sniffing and licking me." The dog wagged his tail and hung his head, another mournful howl issuing from deep within the massive body. "See what I mean?"

"No, I don't see what you mean. He loves you and doesn't understand why you're acting so strange."

"Ah-ha." She waved a finger at him. "So now you admit it's strange." Allie wanted to stop, but couldn't. She felt like a fool, trying to be something she wasn't, then having a stupid dog expose her.

"No, I'm not admitting anything. Allie, if you'll just get off your high horse for a minute, you of all people should see the humor in Chev's actions."

"As the Queen would say, we are not amused." She started yanking things off the table and carrying them to the kitchen, flipping on all the overhead lights. "So much for candlelight and romance."

He caught her as she turned from the sink. "Allie, listen to me. I don't want you to change. I like you just the way you are."

"That's impossible." She yanked open the dishwasher and started throwing dishes into it.

"Why the hell is it impossible?"

"Because you have a political future. Politicians have wimpy little wives who stand beside them in designer clothes and smile a lot. They don't have wives who stand beside them with dog slobbers on their clothes." She slammed the dishwasher.

"Some politicians." He caught sight of her flashing eyes and his breath caught. "You're talking about wives again."

"Name two who don't," she demanded, ignoring his last remark.

Frank took two deep breaths and wanted to shake some sense into her silk-clad little body. "I can't think of any right off hand, but I will."

"I rest my case. So all that could possibly happen

between us is an affair and I can't do that." She started past him toward the table.

He caught her arm and turned her. The air crackled between them. "I'm not asking you to do that."

"Frank, it's hopeless." Her eyes searched his.

"It isn't." He pulled her into his arms, but she remained rigid. "Allie, why can't you just accept that I love you and not try to be something you think I want?"

"Because you couldn't possibly want someone like me. I mean you couldn't possibly want me unless I cleaned up my act. Which I could do, but—"

"I should know what I want. Look, I know there was another lawyer who hurt you. I'm not even sure he is what this is all about. I don't know what he did. If you want me to know, I figure you'll tell me. But I am not him."

"He."

"He?"

"I am not he."

"Oh, great. Just great. I'm talking about our future and she's giving grammar lessons," he muttered in Chevis's direction. "Okay, Allison Tarkington, here's what we are going to do. You are going to go in your bedroom and change into your sweatsuit. I would prefer the green one, but any one will do. I am going to go out the front door, and in exactly five minutes, I am going to ring the door bell and we are going to start this evening all over again."

"You're kidding."

"I am not kidding. I am going to tell you what happened at the office and you are going to tell me how things were at the pound or wherever the hell you were today."

"I was cleaning the stupid house today so you'd think

I was capable of wearing designer clothes and smiling like a wimpy politician's wimpy wife."

"Go. Now. Five minutes." He waited for her to move. "Allie, go or I'll take you in that bedroom and strip you down. I cannot, however, guarantee that I will re-dress you anytime in the forseeable future."

Her eyes became impossibly wide. "You wouldn't."

"Try me." He started toward her, smiling when she started backing toward the hall.

"And people think *I'm* crazy," she muttered.

Frank retired to the front porch to pace and suck in great quantities of cold air—to cool his mind and his body. He was determined to convince her that he loved her and was more than willing to take her in any way, shape, or form. But she was a proud, stubborn woman, and he knew she'd made up her mind that he needed more than she could ever provide. Except, something more kept nagging at his mind. Something else about which she had made up her mind. He paced faster, his heart racing at the thought of that silk dress slithering off her shoulders. He kicked the step.

Frank wasn't at all sure how to unmake her mind, other than carrying her to the bedroom and loving her until she surrendered and believed. And somehow, Frank had never considered himself the Rhett Butler type. He'd have to find another way. When exactly five minutes had passed, Frank had come to the conclusion that he might very well be the Rhett Butler type. At least he damn sure felt like it. He rang the bell and waited, his wanting for her now a living thing. He began to believe she wasn't going to answer and started sizing up the strength of the front door.

When she finally opened the door, she stood, half-hidden behind it. She wore an old gray sweatsuit. "The green one is dirty." The old sweatsuit had shrunk with many washings.

He stopped and looked at her delicious curves under the material and groaned, then walked into the hall to be greeted by Chevis as if he'd just arrived after a long absence. Stooping to pet the dog, he looked at Allie. "Much better, right, Chev?"

Allie stalked down the hall in front of them, muttering to herself about the whole world being crazy.

Frank caught up to her in the kitchen and took her face in his hands. His lips teased hers until she began to respond. As her arms circled him, he pulled her tight, letting his hands make lazy circles on her back while he kissed her until he thought he couldn't stand it any more. As her body arched against him, he felt her hands under his jacket and moaned. "Allie, I love you." Her response was lost in another long, searching, kiss.

When his control was near the edge, he stepped back, a thrill running through him as he saw the desire burning brightly in her eyes. Looking at her moist, kiss-swollen lips, his control wavered. His eyes searched hers for a sign, and when he started to speak, she brushed two fingers against his lips.

"I don't guess you'd like the rest of your brandy, would you?" she said, her voice low and husky.

Her husky voice caused him to groan again. "I can't possibly have any brandy left. I just got here, remember?" He trailed kisses down her jawline and felt her tremble. "You are driving me crazy, Allie."

She stood on tiptoes to whisper in his ear. "The brandy?"

Her soft, sweet breath in his ear pushed him to the edge. "I don't want brandy, Allie, I want you." His lips found hers, hot, wanting.

"Frank, we shouldn't . . ."

"You know we should." His hands touched bare skin under the sweatshirt. Sweet, soft, lovely skin.

"But Frank, we . . . I . . . you can't want me. I'm not normal," she wailed. "I'm not like other—"

Frank cut off her protest with a kiss. "Umm. Two lips." He brushed gentle kisses on her eyelids, then her ears. And felt her tremble. "Two eyes, two ears. Everything normal so far."

"Frank, I'm not talking about that kind of normal." She backed toward the refrigerator and he trapped her there. Her heart was pounding in her ears.

He touched each of her fingers to his lips. "She's got all her fingers," he murmured in her ear, then kissed her throat. "Oh, she's got a very strong pulse."

When she moaned and sought his lips, his passion exploded, his kiss long, searching, demanding. "I want you, Allie. More than I've ever wanted anyone. Love me."

Allie pressed against him, her doubts scattered to the winds. "Oh, yes, Frank, yes." She touched his face with gentle fingertips as if to memorize every inch.

"And just when I was going to see if you had the right number of toes," he said, his voice heavy with desire. With that, Frank swooped her into his arms and carried her down the hallway to where her bedroom must be. He took her through the open door and gently laid her on the bed, sinking with her, afraid to let go.

He showered her face with tender kisses, then moved to her neck and ears. She shivered when his tongue touched her ear. "Allie, Allie, how can I want you so much? You're sure, sweetheart?" Frank knew if she said no, he would die.

"I'm sure," she murmured in his ear.

Frank released her and slid his hands under her shirt, marvelling at the velvety skin which he knew would be creamy white. He sucked in air when he realized she had nothing on under the shirt. His heart soared as he realized she had known what would happen. She wanted him. His hands touched her perfect breasts and with one motion he slid the shirt over her head, then sat back to look at her.

The stained glass shade from the bedside lamp cast gold and lilac shadows on her skin, making it glow. He touched her breast, then bent to kiss it. He felt her hands unbutton his shirt and reach in to touch his skin. Hardly taking his lips from their journey over her breasts and stomach, he managed to slide out of his clothes. "You are so lovely, so lovely."

Allie pulled him down beside her, her sweatpants cast aside in a heap. Her hands caressed his back, then his chest, sliding through the downy blond mat, stroking the long, lithe muscles of his body. "Oh, Frank, you are nice."

He pulled her against him and felt their bodies meld together. "Sweetheart, we are nice together." Her response was lost in his hot kisses, demanding now. "I love you, Allie."

Frank trailed hot kisses down her breastbone and paused to memorize her flat stomach with his lips, then continued his exploration down her thighs. When he had started back up the other thigh, she buried her hands in his thick hair, seeking his face.

She held his face in her hands, branding each bit of his face with her own burning kisses, her desire as urgent as his. She felt the tension in his body as she arched against him, anxious to feel his hard body touching hers from head to toe. When she felt his weight, she clung to him, pulling him tighter, reveling in his strength.

Their need was great as they gave the gift of love, soaring with the eagles, riding the wind to the far ends of the earth and beyond.

Frank lay holding her, unable to comprehend the experience. It was beyond anything he had ever imagined possible. If he lived to be a hundred, he would never get enough of loving her. He touched her face. "You are an incredible woman, Allison Tarkington."

She smiled lazily, her eyes half-closed in satisfaction. "You're not so bad yourself, Franklin Wade."

He nipped at her neck with his lips. "I can get better. With practice." He felt her hands stroke his ribcage and flinched. "That tickles."

"Ummm. I love to torment people who are ticklish." Her hands raced over his body.

He rolled over, half-covering her body with his, kissing her until her hands stroked instead of tickled. He knew that if he didn't get up now, he might never get up. And while her passion had matched his, he didn't want to overwhelm her with the intensity of his need for her. "Now, how about that brandy?"

She nibbled at his chin. "I wonder if Chev could bring it in here?"

He laughed and playfully swatted her rump. "Somehow, I don't think Chev would be very good with crystal. Either we go get the brandy or we stay here. Forever." His lips found hers again, moist, seeking, wanting. His kisses were gentle and knowing, yet the urgency came again, causing him to pull away. "Forever, love."

"In that case..." While Frank dressed, she slipped on an emerald green velour robe and floated into the

Cupid's Campaign

kitchen, feeling as if she were walking on air. Allie had never experienced such passion and love in her life as she had felt with Frank. It thrilled her, yet scared her. As she heard his footsteps in the hall, she wondered what on earth they could possibly talk about after such an experience. Allie felt a twinge of embarrassment, knowing she had to face him in the harsh light of the kitchen with her face still red and swollen from his loving.

As he walked into the kitchen, she turned and filled the snifters they had emptied so long ago. She'd pulled her hair back with a scarf, but wisps curled around her face.

He motioned her into the living room, sensing her conflicting thoughts. She took the sofa and he took the rocker, knowing he could not make any sense whatsoever if he were touching her. He would turn their minds to business and put her mind at ease. He hoped. "I was going to talk to Max today, but he was out."

"So, what now?" She watched him over the rim of her snifter.

"I haven't decided. I still think I should."

She leaned forward. "Frank, he'll warn them. They'll ship the dogs out sooner." She started to get up, but he reached over and laid a hand on her arm. She would not meet his eyes. "Or kill them."

"I filled out the arrest warrant. Ken will pick them up Monday morning." Frank stared into the amber liquid.

"Why do we have to wait till Monday?"

"Because Ken is out till then, and I'm not sure who else to trust." And maybe that would solve the problem of whether or not to talk to Max. He wouldn't see Max before then.

"There must be someone." Her voice was tinged with impatience.

"Allie, you're the one who told me everyone is involved. Which I don't believe, but it's possible someone else may be involved. Look, even if I do tell Max and he is involved, he couldn't afford to warn them. It would implicate him."

Allie slumped back to the sofa. "Sorry I don't share your optimism."

"The other reason is that the judge won't be available until Monday to sign the warrant."

"Can't we barge into his house or something? Perry Mason wouldn't wait for Monday."

He moved to the sofa. "I am not Perry Mason and no, we can't. Monday will be plenty of time." He put his arm around her and pulled her close. She snuggled against him and he knew her momentary discomfort was over. "Now, about this awful pain called love that I seem to be suffering from." He drew his name on her thigh with his finger.

Allie sighed. "Frank, changing clothes and making love doesn't alter the fact that I am unsuitable for you." There was a sadness in her voice which hadn't been there before.

"Allie, I am very much in love with you and you might feel the same if you would admit it." He brushed a kiss on her nose. "I want to marry you."

Allie turned to look at him, eyes wide. "That's impossible and I'm going to forget you said that. And I can't admit I love you. If I did, then some fine morning you would realize what I've been trying to tell you and it would be too late for me." Allie knew now how much she loved him and wanted to tell him she just couldn't stand the hurt if he left her. Or when he left her. In spite

Cupid's Campaign 147

of his declarations and the intensity of his lovemaking, Allie was afraid. More afraid than she had been before. Afraid he would realize he needed a wife who could be an asset to him, not someone who spent her time making waves at city hall. And afraid of something even more basic—the problem of her animals.

Frank rolled his eyes toward the ceiling. "You are, without a doubt, the most obstinate, luscious woman I have ever met in my life." He frowned and toyed with a string on her old sweatshirt. "That's only part of it, isn't it? Why don't you tell me what you're really afraid of?"

"Frank, believe me, I'm doing what is best for you. Allie regretted their lovemaking now. It had been a mistake, just as she had known it would be. Her memories of that love would make the parting too painful to bear.

"Dammit, I don't need someone to look out after my best interests. My mother still does that full time."

"Frank, we've been thrown together, ships in the night and all that stuff. After Monday, we won't have anything in common."

"I don't believe you can say that after what just happened between us, Allie." He hugged her close, sensing the loss already, knowing their passion had shaken her as much as it had him. She was afraid, but there was something else. Suddenly he knew. "It's the animals, isn't it? You think I couldn't put up with the animals, don't you?" He shifted to the edge of the sofa, turning toward her. He saw the answer in her eyes. "Allie, why would you think that?"

She looked away from him. "Frank, it's the way things are. It's fine now, but there would come a day when it would be too much—when I would have to choose between them and you."

"No, Allie, I couldn't do that to you."

She smiled sadly. "Frank, one night I would sit up with a sick dog and you would begin to resent it. The next time would be worse. Then pretty soon..."

He took her shoulders. "Allie, give me a little credit. I could never resent the time you gave to a sick animal." Hurt edged his voice.

"Frank, I want to believe, now more than ever, but I've seen it happen too many times—to other people in the same line of work. I just couldn't make that choice. I don't want to love you, then somewhere down the road have to make that choice."

Frank stood up and stared down at her. "I'm leaving now. When you come to your senses, you'll know you love me as much as I love you. You'll know we belong together and that to keep us apart would be like wrenching the sun from the roses. I'm going to forget what you said just now. But I'm not going to forget the wonder of what happened to us tonight. And neither are you. I love you. I want to love you forever." He waited for her to reach for him, but she didn't. "I'll see you tomorrow."

Allie heard the pain in his voice and cursed herself. She looked up and saw the pain in his eyes. Had she been totally wrong about him? In that moment, she knew she had, but the apology stuck in her throat as she remembered she had to keep him away for a day or two. "I have things to do tomorrow and Sunday, Frank. I have to... take some animals to new homes."

He started back toward her, then stopped. "I'll call you, then." With that, Frank stalked to the door, the ache already threatening to rip his heart apart.

As Frank drove home, he almost wept with longing —longing for a lifetime of what he'd tasted tonight. Perhaps he'd been too harsh, but he didn't know what else to do. He didn't know how to make her see that her compassion was so important to him. He would call her tomorrow, after she'd had a chance to sleep on it. If she hurt as much in a night as he'd hurt in a few minutes, she would see.

Chapter Eleven

FRANK WATCHED the sun come up as he drove his sports car entirely too fast to his hometown of Lamar. He wasn't sure why he'd decided to go there, but he could no longer stand the sterile quietness of his apartment, and it was in the opposite direction from Allie's house. No danger of just happening to drive by, then happening to see a light, then...

He automatically turned on to the street which would take him to his parents' house. He'd planned to stop by and see his mother this morning, but as he neared the house, he realized it would not be a good idea. She would be too full of questions about the Tarkingtons. Questions he could no more answer than the questions he had wrestled with all night. Questions like how could he convince Allie that he could love her and all the animals she chose to drag home? And how could he make her see that they belonged together in a way not even he could begin to explain. Particularly after last night. He hung a left and headed back to the highway.

Wheeling into a truck stop, he drank a lot of strong

coffee and pushed a lot of eggs around on a sturdy truck stop plate. He finally pushed the plate aside and left, driving his car too fast back to Reedsville and to the courthouse. There was plenty of work to do, and maybe if he got immersed in his work, he could forget about his problems. Surely, after a day or two, Allie would see everything as clearly as he saw it.

Even the offices looked sterile and quiet when he entered the dim reception area, which should have been no surprise considering it was Saturday. The arrest warrant lying in its neat folder on his desk seemed to mock him and remind him of Allie more than of the man for whom the warrant had been written.

He stared at the phone, aching to hear her voice. As he picked up a file, his hands shook with a need to touch her satiny skin, taste her sweet lips, feel the passion of her response. He sat for long moments, savoring the memory of her.

Unable to concentrate on any of his cases, he busied himself with letters and housekeeping chores. After a few hours of work, he felt better—not good, but better —as long as he didn't look at the phone. If he looked at the phone, he wanted to pick it up and call Allie.

Frank looked up in surprise when he heard the outer door of the office open, then decided one of the other assistant prosecutors must be playing catch up, too. His own door was closed, so he couldn't see who it was and didn't go look because he was in no mood today to visit with anyone.

A little before noon, the vague restlessness which had sent him out driving earlier crept back into Frank's mind and body. He'd done all the busywork he could handle for one day. As he stepped out into the unlighted hallway, he couldn't see any lights in any of the offices.

As he passed the receptionist's desk, he glanced down the other hallway and saw light coming from Max's office.

Frank stood for a moment, drumming his fingers on the desk, wondering what Max was doing there on a Saturday. It was more than unusual, it was unheard of unless he was on a big case, and right now, they didn't have any cases like that.

As Frank started to leave, all the rage and pent up anger over the dogs and Allie's seeming rejection swept over him. He knew he should leave, started to leave, but couldn't. He had to let Max know what a creep he had for a brother-in-law. Mostly, he had to know if Max was involved. He walked into Max's office, rapping the open door with his knuckles as he entered.

The older man looked up at Frank with a frown. "Hi, Frank. Working on Saturday? Well, haven't seen much of you lately."

Frank closed the door and stood with his back against it. "I've had some things to do, Max." Now that he was here, he wasn't sure whether he should say anything about Lonnie or not. When he looked at Max sitting there, he knew his rage wasn't against Max, but... Frank decided to tell him. He did owe the man something. "Max, I have reason to believe Lonnie is involved in stealing dogs for a lab in Dunbar. I also have reason to believe he may be a part owner in that lab."

Max started to jump up, then sat back, hands behind his head. His face was a study in control, only a slight red flush betraying the fact that anything might be amiss. When he spoke, his voice was quiet. "She got to you, didn't she, Franky, boy."

"No one got to me, Max," he said in a quiet voice.

Cupid's Campaign   153

The silence of the office was broken only by Max's measured breathing. "Max, are you involved in it?"

A harsh laugh filled the office. "I don't think that's any of your business, boy. Just why are you telling me all this? Why didn't you just have Lonnie arrested and be done with it?"

"I thought I owed you, Max." Frank held his breath, waiting, willing Max to deny it, to explain it.

Max rose and came around the desk. "I'll tell you why you didn't. Because you don't have one damn shred of evidence, that's why. You're fishing, Frank." The flush spread and turned his face an angry red.

Frank saw the anger in Max's face and his refusal to meet Frank's eyes and knew his boss was involved. Maybe not actively, but he had condoned it. Frank expelled his breath, then inhaled deeply. Anger turned to rage in a flash. "You're wrong, Max. I thought you should know before I had the arrest warrant served."

"Bull! You don't have enough for a warrant and you know it." He shook a stubby finger at Frank. "You got two choices, Frank. You learn to play ball and you'll make it in politics. Otherwise, you walk outta here and go to your flaky little broad and forget about being prosecutor. Your choice."

Frank stood with clenched fists behind his back, the cold rage eating at his belly. A rage at the man standing in front of him, a rage at himself for being around corruption for five years and never smelling it. When he spoke again, his voice had the satin of polished steel. "You're wrong, Max. I'm going to bring all of them down, then I'm going to be the next prosecutor. Then I'm going to marry that 'flaky little broad'. If you're smart, Max, you'll resign today—for health reasons."

Max roared with harsh laughter. "You're finished,

Franky, boy. Finished." He turned to pick up the phone. "You'll be lucky if they'll even let you practice law when I get through with you."

Frank yanked the door open and started out into the hall, afraid if he didn't leave, he would lose his temper and do something he might regret—like punch Max in the nose. He turned and shook a finger at Max. "Don't warn them, Max. Just don't do it, or I'll take you down hard, so help me God."

"Franky boy, do you really think a man can live on a lousy prosecutor's salary? Oh, I used to be full of fire too, until the kids' teeth needed braces and there wasn't enough damn money. Do you know what salary I started at?" His voice held a mixture of anger and self-pity.

Frank left the building, unwilling to listen to the excuses. Public servants who went bad always had excuses. His body shook with anger as he turned his car toward home. He wished to hell Ken was available, he would have the warrant served right now. Ken would know who in the sheriff's office to trust. Frank raged inwardly that he would even be thinking things like that. A few days ago, it would never have occurred to him that the sheriff's office might be tainted. But then, it would never have occurred to him that Max was involved in such a dirty business.

He didn't think even Max would dare to deepen his involvement by warning Lonnie off. Even if he did, Frank would find Lonnie. If not Monday, another day, but he would find him. And he would have to tell Allie what he had done. At least it would be a good excuse to call her.

Allie picked up the phone on the second ring and Frank felt a surge of love and desire when he heard her voice. He wanted to believe she'd been near the phone,

Cupid's Campaign   155

waiting. When he realized she was still waiting for someone to speak, he said, "Hi."

"Hi."

Frank thought her voice sounded a little strained, and he hoped it was from a bad night—a bad night of hurting and wanting him like he'd wanted her. "How are you?"

"Fine. You?"

He heard Chevis howl in the background. "Fine. What does Chev want?"

"Who knows? Uh, Frank, I'm sorry about last night." A pause. "I mean right before you left."

Relief swept through Frank. She didn't regret their loving. "Yeah, me too. I wondered if you wanted to—"

"But it still doesn't change the basic problem, Frank." Her voice cracked.

Panic replaced the relief. "Allie, what do you mean it doesn't change the basic problem. We don't have a basic problem." He heard her sigh.

"We do. You just won't admit it. We shouldn't have let it go this far, it just makes things harder. Frank, I've seen it time and time again." Her voice seemed to break.

"So, we'll just be the exception to the rule." Why couldn't she believe him? He felt the hurt and pain stab at him.

"Look, Frank, maybe we could, maybe not. But we have to stop right where we are. I can't... I have to have time. It's not something I can just rush into. It would be a major life change. For both of us."

"I know, honey, I know. How about dinner tonight and we can hash it out." He held his breath, willing her to say yes.

"I don't know..."

He could feel her waver. Maybe he could convince her with business. They could talk about the case. "I saw Max at the office this morning." She would have to try and convince him to move ahead with the warrant. She could do it over dinner.

She seemed to stop breathing. "And?"

"I had to tell him, Allie."

"Frank, he'll warn them, you know he will."

"He won't. I made it pretty clear what would happen if he did." No response. "Allie, come to dinner with me tonight."

"I can't Frank. I just can't tonight." There was a long pause. "I have things to do."

"Oh." Frank ached in his deepest being. He couldn't let her go so easily. "Dammit, woman, I love you. And I love your zoo. And I want to marry you. And I'm going to keep after you till I get all of you. But you have to realize what we have. So you call me when you decide." He thought he heard a sharp intake of breath from her.

"Frank, I have to go. I'll talk to you later."

Frank sat listening to the dial tone.

Allie was in the truck headed for Dunbar when the sun settled behind the trees. She could still hear the pain in Frank's voice, a pain which matched that which she'd felt all night and all day.

During the long night, she'd come to see just how much she loved Frank, and she knew she would take the chance with him. She'd thought she loved him before last night's magic, but now there was no doubt left. She'd heard the pain, wanted to tell him, but she couldn't—yet. Not until Dottie was taken care of. If he was willing to try and put up with her and her menagerie, then she was willing to limit the number of animals and help him in any way she could with his career, including wimpy smiles and designer dresses. She'd just have to find a cure for dog slobbers.

That is, if she hadn't run him off for good. She'd been ready to go out with him and plead her case for one last time, give him a chance to back out. After all, she wanted him to know exactly what he was trying to get involved in. She had lost her heart to him, but to have him for a while, then have the animal business creep in would be unbearable. And if they made love again, there would be no backing out. She knew that.

But when he'd told her about Max, she'd known what she had to do and it couldn't wait till Sunday night.

Frank might believe in honor among thieves or whatever, but she had no such illusions. There was no doubt in Allie's mind that when dark came, those animals would either be shipped out or destroyed. And because she loved Frank and respected his belief in the legal system, she couldn't ask him to help her.

Allie knew he *would* help, even though what she had in mind was illegal. He would help because he loved her. But if Allie was going to try and make a go of the relationship, she couldn't ask him to break the law. It was going to be hard enough to ever face him again. As she turned off the highway onto the dirt road, she just hoped she would have a chance to explain to him why she had to do what she was doing.

She parked the truck well back from the chain link gate, in the turnaround Frank had used that night which now seemed so long ago. Following the edge of the woods, she came to the fence and followed it further into the woods, hoping their security wouldn't be quite so good farther from the front of the building.

The area was deserted as she turned the corner of the fence and stood looking at the back of the building. She shifted the heavy backpack, filled with the various and sundry tools she'd gathered up. There was just enough of a moon for her to see the fence clearly as it stretched before her. No breaks in it. She followed it another fifty feet before she found an area where the clips which held the fencing to the posts were broken and the fence was bowed out and loose.

She quickly pulled the fence away from the post and slipped under it. It was a tight squeeze and she didn't think she'd ever manage to herd a bunch of dogs through the hole, but she would worry about that later. She'd brought bolt cutters and could cut the chain on the gate to get out. She just didn't want it cut now in case anyone showed. The time it would take them to unlock the gate would give her warning and time to escape—maybe.

Allie crept up to the back of the building and peered in a dirty window. The building was totally dark and she couldn't see a thing. After quickly checking the door and finding it locked, she decided the window was the best bet. Turning her face away and closing her eyes, she jammed her backpack against the window. The shattering glass sounded like an explosion in the still night.

When the dogs started barking in response to the breaking window, Allie thought her heart would jump right out her mouth. She broke the rest of the glass out and crawled through, directing the weak beam of a small flashlight in front of her. She'd never been able to figure out why flashlight batteries failed just when one needed them the most. She decided in that moment that she would never succeed in a life of crime. She would have heart failure before she could do the deed.

She talked quietly, hoping the damn dogs would shut up before they roused the whole county. But they just got louder, and she heard Dottie howling louder than the rest. She smiled in relief as she followed the beam of the flashlight around the room. Now if she could just get them out. Two walls of the room were lined with dog cages, most of which were empty. Cabinets and shelves lined one wall. A stainless steel table sat in the middle of the room with lamps hanging above it.

Still speaking softly, she started toward the cages, trying to ignore the warning bells clanging in her mind. She'd imagined she heard the gate, but in the din of the dogs, she couldn't be sure. She stopped a minute, listening, but knew it was hopeless. All she could hear was the dogs—and her own heart pounding. She just had to get the dogs and get out.

She ran down the line of cages, snapping open doors, hoping like hell the dogs would be glad enough to be free that they would follow her. She had nylon leashes in her pack for the trip back to the truck, but she sensed that there was no time for that now. As she bent to unsnap the last cage, the bright operating lights flashed on, blinding her. As she started to turn, something fell on her head and she slipped into darkness again.

Chapter Twelve

THE RED SPORTS car shone brighter than the day it had come off the line. Frank had washed it, then polished it until he was afraid he would rub the paint off it. In spite of the cold, he'd worked up a sweat trying to spread the wax, but at least the project had managed to kill most of the afternoon.

He'd been so sure Allie would be back to her bright, snappy self today. So sure she would have thought things over and seen they had to spend their lives together. And for a moment, he'd known things would work out. He'd heard the uncertainty in her voice as she stated her case against a relationship.

Then she'd receded back into her shell and refused to talk to him again. Something about that nagged at Frank, but he couldn't quite put his finger on it. Frank studied his reflection in the hood of the car. He must have been crazy to tell her she would have to call him. She was a proud woman and she might never call.

Frank went into his apartment and mixed a stiff drink, then decided he didn't want it. He paced the

Cupid's Campaign 161

floor, staring at the phone, willing it to ring, but it sat silent. Finally picking it up and dialing her number, he wondered what the hell he would do if she said no again. He wasn't sure he could handle it. But the chance never came as the phone rang and rang. She probably wasn't answering, he thought, slamming the receiver back in its cradle.

He turned on the sports channel and watched impossibly tall men make impossible shots with a basketball, but didn't really care. He called again, no answer. He began to worry.

Then her sudden coolness struck Frank again and a thought occurred to him. What if she'd decided to do something really stupid, like go to that lab and try to rescue Dottie? Frank sat bolt upright in his chair and let that idea percolate for a few minutes. That would explain why she didn't want to see him tonight. That would explain why she'd been almost ready to go with him until he mentioned Max. That would explain a lot of things, Frank thought as he grabbed his coat and ran to his car.

When he got to Allie's house, his worry turned to fear when he didn't see her truck. What if she was right about Max? If Max had warned Lonnie, and Allie had gone to rescue Dottie, they just might all end up at the lab at the same time.

Frank pounded on the door trying to convince himself that her truck was in the shop or loaned out or something. But a minute later, he was on his way to Elspeth's, telling himself that she was probably there having dinner. He pulled into her drive just as the sun disappeared behind the trees in Elspeth's back yard. Her truck wasn't there.

Frank fought to compose himself as he waited for the

door to open. He didn't want to alarm the old woman. He smiled, confidently he hoped, when she opened the door.

"Oh, hello, Mr. Wade." She peered around him in the dusk. "Where are they?"

Fear gripped Frank's belly like a vicious talon. "Where are who, Mrs. Tarkington?"

"Why Allie and Dottie, of course."

Frank took her arm and led her into the lighted kitchen. "Have you seen Allie, Mrs. Tarkington?"

The old woman frowned, worry lines creasing her plump face. "Well, of course. But I thought you were with her."

Frank gently led her to a chair and seated her. "Everything's fine. Just tell me when you saw her and what she said." He sat close to her, holding one of her hands.

"Oh, dear. I knew something wasn't right. I just knew it. Allison's done something very silly and dangerous, hasn't she?" She looked at Frank with pleading eyes.

Frank took a deep breath, refusing to agree with Elspeth even though he knew she was right. Now he had to get what information she had and get it quickly. "When was she here?"

"Late this afternoon. She was most distraught. She didn't say, but I got the definite impression you and she had had a spat." She clutched Frank's hand. "Oh, Franklin, she'd been so happy this week. Well, not about Dottie, of course, but I've seen the way you look at each other." She smiled. "I may be an old woman, but I still remember about love."

Frank's heart caught in his throat. Elspeth knew Allie loved him, even if Allie didn't know it yet. At least that was a start. Then the reality of her situation came crashing down on him again. "Mrs. Tarkington, tell me what Allie said."

"Well, it was rather peculiar, as I said. She was quite adamant about going to get Dottie tonight. She said she would be back here soon. I just assumed you were going with her. In fact, I asked, but all she said was that she didn't have anything to lose by going tonight. Do you know what she meant?"

Frank felt the fear settle in his belly and start growing. "I probably do, Mrs. Tarkington. I probably do. May I use your phone?"

"Of course. She will be all right, won't she, Franklin?" She blinked and a solitary tear rolled down her cheek.

Frank brushed a kiss on the old woman's cheek and squeezed her hand. "Yes, ma'am, she will, if I have to move heaven and earth."

Frank quickly dialed Ken's home number, hoping against hope that Ken had not left town for the weekend. After pleading with Ken's wife that it was an emergency, the chief came on the line.

"Dammit, Frank, it's Saturday night and I'm off this weekend. This better be important."

Frank quickly explained what he knew and what he suspected. "Can you meet me at the courthouse in fifteen minutes, Ken?" There was a short pause.

"Yeah. I'll have the sheriff meet us at the lab. You got the arrest warrant signed?"

"I'll have it signed on the way. It's all made out." But what if he couldn't find the judge or the court clerk? "We could go without it."

"Be better if we had it all nice and legal, Frank."

"See you in a few minutes, Ken, and thanks."

"You owe me one, Frank."

Frank hurried back to the kitchen. "Mrs. Tarkington, do you know Judge Macklin?"

Elspeth beamed, anxious to help. "Of course I know William. He was a great friend of Matthew's, Mr. Tarkington."

Frank took her hand again, hoping he could convey what he wanted with none of the panic he felt. "Could you call Judge Macklin and tell him that we suspect Allie may be in a bit of trouble. Tell him the police chief and I are on our way to check it out, but that I need an arrest warrant signed. We'll stop by his house in a few minutes."

"Yes, I'll call right now."

Frank saw the determination on her face and knew she would find Judge Macklin if she had to track him to the ends of the earth. "And don't worry. We'll make sure nothing happens to Allie." He gave her a reassuring smile and wished he felt as confident as he was trying to make her feel.

Ken was waiting when Frank got to the courthouse. The warrant retreived from his desk, the men were silent as the police cruiser raced toward Dunbar after a quick stop at Judge Macklin's house.

Frank's heart almost stopped when he saw Allie's truck pulled into a little side road off the dirt road which led to the lab. It started again, pounding and racing this time when they rounded the bend in the road and stopped in front of the gate, which now yawned open, the chain and padlock cast aside.

When Frank started to leap from the car, Ken stopped him, a heavy hand on his arm. "Best wait for the sheriff, Frank."

"Ken, she might be in there, hurt." Or dead, he

Cupid's Campaign 165

thought, pain stabbing at him like a hot lance. He would never forgive himself if anything had happened to Allie. He should have helped her, to hell with his precious law.

"Frank, it looks deserted, but a lot of good men have been killed barging into deserted buildings." At that moment, another police car skidded to a halt beside them. The red and blue lights flashed an eerie pattern across the dull metal of the building.

Frank waited impatiently as Ken and the sheriff conferred. Ken climbed back into the cruiser and drove through the gate, the sheriff's car behind. They circled the building at a slow crawl, spotlights raking the building with white beams. Ken stopped the car at the back of the building when the spotlight touched the broken window. Both men saw a small dog huddled beside a door which stood slightly ajar.

Ken put the frightened dog into the car, then carefully opened the door to the building, standing to one side. Frank saw that both men had drawn their guns. Ken motioned for Frank to stand aside as he slipped into the building. Frank could hardly breathe by the time he saw lights come on in the building. He stepped through the gaping door.

The officers stood in the lighted room, looking around, their guns still at ready, although it was obvious the place was deserted. File cabinet drawers lay scattered on the floor, the contents hauled away by whomever had been there first. Several dogs whined from open cages and shadowy corners.

Tears came to Frank's eyes when he realized they were too late. No Allie, no Dottie. Either they were dead or the men had taken them along, possibly as hostages. Frank was barely aware of Ken's hand on his shoulder.

"They haven't been gone long, Frank. We'll find them."

Frank nodded, vaguely aware of the sheriff's voice calling on a car radio for a lab crew. "I should have listened to her, Ken."

"Frank, you didn't know. Why don't you wait in the car while we see what we can find. Then I'll take you back to town."

Frank shook his head and wandered around the room, peering into the cages at the frightened dogs, hoping one would be an almost Dachshund. None were. He wondered why the dogs had taken refuge back in the cages instead of slipping out of the building. The only explanation he could think of was that some terrible struggle had taken place, frightening them back into their temporary homes.

Suddenly the quiet was broken by a muffled pounding somewhere in the building. Frank stiffened and watched the lawmen converge on a door which might be a storeroom or an office, guns drawn again. Ken gingerly tried the door knob and found the door locked. Slipping a thin sliver of plastic in beside the door frame, the sheriff threw the door open, then filled the door with his body, gun at the ready position. When nothing happened, he hit a light switch beside the door, then lowered his gun.

Frank heard the sheriff chuckle and rushed through the door, almost knocking the man off his feet. He froze at the sight which greeted him. Allie was bound and gagged, half-sitting, half-lying on an old cot. A funny looking very fat dog was struggling to maintain a place on her lap, although actually the dog was more on

Cupid's Campaign 167

Allie's stomach. Above the gag, Allie's green eyes flashed and danced.

The two lawmen backed out of the room as Frank reached her in one step. He whipped off the gag before he gathered her in his arms. "Oh, Allie, I thought . . . I thought something had happened."

Allie spit out the remaining bits of cloth and looked up at him. "What are you doing here?"

Frank could have cried for joy at her familiar demanding question. "I just happened to be in the neighborhood . . . I thought I'd stop by and rescue you."

Allie struggled to sit up, jutting her chin out and trying to look indignant. "I don't know what you're worried about, I'll have you know Dottie and I have everything under control."

Frank laughed, the icy fear draining from his body like a river as he untied her. "Well, I guess I could just put the gag back on and go home."

"You wouldn't dare."

"Then show a little proper appreciation." He started to untie her hands, then stopped. "By the way, have you given up those silly ideas about me and the animals and commitment and such?"

"Franklin Wade, you untie me. Right now." Then she grinned. "Well, I did have a little time for thinking tonight."

Frank knelt on the cot and reached behind her. Her voice and eyes had told him what he needed to know. When her arms were free, they circled him, clinging. "Dammit, woman, you took ten years off my life tonight."

"It didn't exactly *add* any years to mine," she muttered into his chest. "I love you, Frank. I love you so much. I thought I might never see you again, and I knew I'd hurt you, and I didn't know what to do about it, and I didn't—"

He placed gentle fingers on her lips and kissed her forehead. "I know. We were both a little crazy, but let's just forget about all that. I have you now and you're not going to get away this time." He cut off her reply with a long, hungry kiss.

It was close to midnight when Frank wheeled the old truck into Elspeth's drive. They had delivered Boopsie and Oliver and Greywolf back to their grateful owners. The remaining dogs were bedded down in the camper. Only Dottie remained in the cab, ensconced between Allie and Frank, tail wagging, tongue hanging out for an occasional lick. Frank and Allie had, between stops, explained all the misunderstandings to each other and laughed them off. It all seemed so silly and so simple now.

When the truck stopped, the back door of the house opened and Elspeth, Gladys, and Triola tumbled down the steps like animated characters in a cartoon. Dottie sailed over Allie's legs and out the open door, howling like a banshee, headed for Elspeth. All three ladies were weeping profusely by the time Frank and Allie got to them.

"Oh, Franklin, Allie, how can I ever thank you?" Elspeth wailed.

"I'm just glad we got to them in time, Gran," Allie said, bending to hug Elspeth, who was on her knees hugging Dottie. She explained that Boopsie and crew were safe, too. "All those men wanted were the records and files. Of course, with Dottie snarling and biting, and with me threatening, well, they were afraid to take the dogs."

Frank grinned and winked at the ladies. "Dottie may have snarled and bitten, but I think our detective was conked on the head early on so she couldn't identify them."

Allie shot Frank a withering glance. "It was my rescue, I'll tell it however I want."

Elspeth sighed and tried to get up. "Oh, dear. I don't think I can get up."

"Old women shouldn't ever get down on their knees, Elspeth," Triola chimed in righteously.

"Oh, pooh, Triola," Gladys snipped. "We're not old women, we're just a little long in the tooth as my daddy used to say."

Frank and Allie got Elspeth up and refused an invitation to tea, pleading fatigue. Elspeth caught the look they exchanged, smiled knowingly and patted each in turn. "Thank you, children. You've made an old woman very happy tonight." Tears glistened in her eyes.

It was well into the wee hours when Allie and Frank got all the dogs settled, then retired to her living room with brandy and coffee and an overenthusiastic Chevis. Frank finally began to relax, the tension draining from his body as he sat watching the woman he loved and all her animals. He knew that soon he would pick her up and carry her to the bedroom and love her, but first they had to get rid of the last of the tension and fear of the evening. He wanted this night to be perfect. "Explain one thing. You told me early on that Dottie only had five days. So why were Boopsie and Oliver still there?"

Allie smiled and stretched. "Well, it did get you moving, didn't it?"

"Do you mean you just told me that?" He frowned at her.

"Actually, no. They're registered dogs, and sometimes research labs want several of a certain breed. So they hold dogs until they can meet the order. Otherwise, five working days or a week is about it."

Allie sipped brandy and stroked a cat. "What will happen to those men, Frank?"

Frank pushed Chev aside and pulled Allie close. "Assault, theft, crossing state lines with stolen goods, whatever else I can think of by morning."

"And Max?"

"He played the game, now he has to pay the piper. They'll all go away for a good while, sweet." He nuzzled her neck. "Then, of course, I have you for breaking and entering, trespassing, and a few other little things."

"You wouldn't dare." Her eyes widened.

"I could get the judge to sentence you to the county jail. That way, I could see you every day, and I'd know you were safe and out of trouble." He trailed a gentle finger down her sweatshirt. "After all, a man running for public office can't show any preference to criminals."

"Well, at least *I* rescued the dogs. It seems all those goons came back for was the files."

"You and the Lone Ranger. No doubt the files were more than slightly incriminating. But we'll find them. If we don't get the files, we have enough. Those stupid creeps saved all the collars they stripped off the dogs. Ken found them in a cabinet. Almost like they were keeping trophies." He felt Allie shudder. Turning to her, he took her snifter and set it on the table. "We are going to get married, aren't we? Soon?"

"I don't know, Frank. I'm willing to try, but I don't think we're ready for that step, yet."

"Umm. Maybe a stretch in the slammer will convince you." He slipped his hand under her shirt and felt her shiver. "Well? Make up your mind. A stretch in the slammer or a lifetime with me." He nibbled at her ear.

"It's awfully hard to make decisions with certain persons munching on my ear." Her fingertips traced an intricate pattern down his chest, unbuttoning buttons on the way.

"Umm. You taste so nice." His nibbling trailed from her ear down her throat. When her hand reached inside his shirt and continued its strange and wonderful pattern, he groaned aloud.

"Shall I quit?" She snatched her hand away, but he captured it and held it to his skin.

"Don't you dare. Ever." He lay down on the sofa and pulled her on top of him, capturing her face in both hands. His lips caressed hers, teasing, gently touching. "I love you, my flaky animal person." He pushed up her shirt so that bare skin slid against bare skin.

"I'm not flaky, you're just very conservative," she teased as her hands stroked his face.

"Ummm. I think we'll just stay right here for the rest of our lives." Frank pulled at her sleeves until her arms came free. Instead of pulling the sweatshirt off over her head, he nuzzled his way under it, trapping himself against her warm breasts.

"Frank, you'll smother." She pulled his shirt free.

"Ummmm. What a way to go." The warm lemony smell and satiny skin caused desire to rip through Frank with an intensity men dream of. He held her legs tight between his, wanting to feel every inch of her body against his. She shivered and pressed against him, her own need matching his. Suddenly, something cold and wet touched Frank's exposed neck. "What—" He turned his head slightly to find himself staring into Chev's bright eyes.

Allie burst out laughing. "I told you it wasn't going to be easy."

Frank gave the dog a serious look. "Old son, I hate to tell you this, but your mistress belongs to me tonight. You'll just have to be brave." With that, he untangled himself and pulled Allie to her feet. At the kitchen door, her sweatshirt fell to the floor and he stopped and pulled her against him as his shirt joined hers. Bare skin touching, their lips met, touching, caressing, probing.

Frank felt an aching gentleness mingle with his overwhelming desire. This was his woman. "Allie, marry me. Now."

Her hands stroked his face. "Chev is not ordained."

"Never a serious bone in your body, woman." He knelt before her, slipping off first one shoe, then the other. His hands stroked her perfect legs, magically taking her jeans with the stroking. He kissed his way up her thighs, over the lace bikinis, up her quivering belly, to rest once again on her lips. With that, he scooped her up and walked oh-so-slowly down the hall, her arms tightly around his neck, their lips barely touching, murmuring words of love and delight.

When they stepped through the door, Chev almost walking on their heels, Frank very politely turned and closed the door in his face. "Sorry, Chev. Go find a kitty." Allie's laugh mingled with Frank's at Chev's disappointed howl disappearing in the direction of the kitchen. Frank set Allie on her feet, and, in one deft motion, the lace lay on the floor and she stood before him, beautiful, perfect, waiting—for the man she loved.

In seconds, Frank stood before her, his strong, lithe

body glowing in the warm light. She stretched her hands out to him. Their fingers entwined, their lips touched.

Frank summoned his control, wanting this moment to last, wanting to savor all of her.

Allie pulled away to gaze again at his wonderful body. The wonderful body which so easily set hers on fire. Unable to wait, she led him toward the bed, her need to feel him against her undeniable. "Maybe you should go to court just like this, Frank. You'd win any case where there were women jurors," she murmured into the warmth of his strong neck.

"Okay. Sure you want me to?" He lay across the bed and pulled her to him.

"Uh-uh. They'd attack you." She nibbled ferociously at his belly, trying to slow the passion, wanting it to last.

"Love me, Allie, now." His lips took hers, the frivolity and waiting over. They gave themselves to the heat, joining together with a savage sweetness which left them breathless as they became one and at last saw a new world heretofore undreamed of.

It was dawn when they stepped out the front door to go retrieve Frank's car. They stood for long moments as the sky changed from blushing pink to fiery red. Frank thought he had never seen a morning more beautiful as he pulled his lady love close and breathed the crisp morning air. He wasn't sure what the future would bring, but he knew just as the morning had been reborn with the sun, he and Allie had been reborn with love.

Epilogue

MARRIED TWO YEARS NOW, Frank and Allison Wade strolled hand in hand among the azaleas, which were in full bloom and providing a riot of color to the carefully manicured backyard of Elspeth's home. Pale green spring grass provided the perfect backdrop for the red and yellow tulips and colorful patio furniture which dotted the yard. A huge birthday cake with one big candle sat on a wrought iron table. Other tables held a variety of inviting goodies.

Allie finally pulled Frank toward a table at the fringe of things so they could watch the party. Her hand touched his on the glass table. She pointed with the other. The guest of honor toddled across the yard, one tiny fist tightly clutching a handful of hair on Chevis's neck. The big dog walked slowly, trying to anticipate the direction his charge might take, urging the baby on with an occasional lick to his face which brought on squeals of laughter from the little boy.

At one point, the wobbly legs tottered and the guest of honor unceremoniously landed on his diapered bottom. Allie laughed and squeezed Frank's hand. Frank laughed with her. Chevis checked to make sure no harm had come to the boy, then presented his neck again and pulled the boy to his feet, resuming their random stroll across the yard. "See Chev smile, Frank?" Allie teased.

"I never knew, until I met you, that an aging German Shepherd could smile."

A fat, mostly Dachshund named Dottie ignored the touching scene in favor of her favorite pastime, food hustling. She had managed to get at least one goodie from every guest on her first round and the afternoon was still young.

Frank and Allie never tired of watching their son, laughing now at his efforts to walk and the permanent worry wrinkles twelve months of baby-sitting had etched on the old dog's face. Chevis had virtually abandoned all the other foundlings to give his full attention to Matthew Wade.

Frank squeezed his wife's hand across the table and sipped wine, listening to the conversation around them. He grinned and motioned with his head toward his mother. "Mother is still trying her best to keep from drooling over your grandmother's house."

"Your mother is a nice lady, Frank. Even if she does think we need to move into a better neighborhood." They both laughed, remembering some of the conversations regarding the problems of moving into a ritzy neighborhood with twenty-some dogs. They had chosen, instead, to remodel Allie's old farmhouse—much more feasible on a prosecutor's salary. They turned at the sound of raised voices.

"He doesn't look a thing like Matthew, he's an almost perfect copy of Elspeth," Triola said indignantly.

Gladys waved a bejeweled arm in the baby's direction. "How would you know, Triola, you can hardly see him. He's Elspeth's Matthew if I ever saw it. That's why they named him after Matthew."

"Elspeth's Matthew had brown hair. And one certainly can't tell how a newborn is going to look."

"I don't give a whit if the baby's hair is green. His face is Matthew's."

Frank and Allie rose and wandered off, holding their laughter until they were a respectable distance from the ladies. If friends and relations were to be taken seriously, their son was a combination of various and sundry body parts gleaned from any number of relatives.

Allie's mother descended on them like a ship under full sail. "He looks exactly like your father, Allison. Oh, Frank, I spoke with some of the women at the country club last week. There's no question but that you're going to be our next attorney general."

Frank smiled and wondered if his campaign for the attorney general's office next year would be quite so filled with excitement as his last campaign had been. Somehow, he didn't think so. Before he could answer, Lisa had latched on to Allie.

"Allie, I'm just green with envy. You know that, don't you? Here you are all settled down and everything. But, you know, I met this professor last week, and, well..."

"Lisa," Allie said sternly. "You went back to school for a master's degree, not a husband."

Lisa hugged her sister. "Just kidding, sis. What I don't understand is how can you possibly abandon all your work here and move to Jackson when Frank wins?"

"Not to worry, Lisa. The election is still a long way

Cupid's Campaign

off. But, I have someone who will stay at the house and take care of things. Besides, think of all the animals in Jackson who need my help." She glanced toward Chevis and her son. "Of course, we'd take Chev and a couple of cats."

"Maybe I'll move there when I finish school. Is the governor married?" Lisa grinned and ducked Allie's playful swat, then became serious. "I really am trying to get my life back in shape, Allie. I don't know how any of you put up with me."

"It wasn't easy."

"Well, you know the strangest thing? It seems like I've inherited Daddy's knack with figures. I may take over his investment firm when I get out." She looked toward their father, who was studying a bed of tulips with great concentration.

Dottie flew by on her begging rounds. She started to sit up and howl, then, noticing that their hands were empty, she rushed toward Elspeth, who had started their way.

"Oh, Dottie, you are a naughty girl. We have to think about our diet. That young vet was most rude to us last week." Dottie showed proper remorse for about two seconds before heading for Gladys and Triola. Elspeth continued toward Frank and Allie. "Isn't Dottie the sweetest thing? I'm so happy for you children. I just wish my Matthew could be here." She smiled and wandered off, shaking her head.

Frank pulled Allie close and nodded toward the house. "You think they would miss us?"

"I don't think anyone even knows we're here." They slipped across the carport and into the big house, Dottie hard on their heels. "It's not suppertime, Dottie. You've eaten so much this afternoon you won't need supper."

"Come on, love." Frank led Allie through the silent house and out the front door, away from the sounds of the party. He motioned her toward the porch swing.

Allie stopped and looked up into his clear blue eyes. "Everything's worked out beautifully hasn't it, Frank? We did good, didn't we?"

"Oh, we did real good, sweetheart. Real good."

"Really," she teased. "We did *really* good."

"Really? I'm *really* going to have to do something about your grammar lessons." Their word games and puns had reached the level of an art. He smothered her response in a kiss. After two years, none of the heat and racing pulse had faded. If anything, his love for her was even greater than it had been. He felt her respond and pulled her closer, marveling at the heat he felt surging through his body.

Allie pulled back when they both felt something burrowing between their legs. Looking down, they saw Dottie, happily sitting on their feet, head up, grinning and panting. Allie shook a finger at the dog. "The next time you get yourself kidnapped, Dottie Do Right, you're on your own. No rescue, no ransom." Dottie howled in protest. Frank and Allie burst into laughter and headed, hand in hand, to the porch swing.

Pulling his lovely bride down onto his lap, Frank set the swing in gentle motion. "With Matt and Chevis holding center stage, I think we can steal a few minutes."

Allie nestled into his arms. "Ummm. We've already stolen a lifetime."

Dottie howled her approval.

SECOND CHANCE AT LOVE

COMING NEXT MONTH

ACCENT ON DESIRE #420
by Christa Merlin

Five-feet-and-feisty investigative reporter Maggie Burton "kidnaps" a sexy stranger's groceries—then learns he's her boss, newspaper publisher Todd Andrews! Todd wants Maggie off his paper and home on his ranch; she uncovers a local scandal, adding new drama to their love...

YOUNG AT HEART #421
by Jackie Leigh

Medical editor Rhetta Stanton falls hard for dazzling heart surgeon "Mac" McHale. He savors feeling young at heart in Rhetta's embrace, but as a widower he knows the pain of loving and losing. The poignant theme is lightened by the author's famed humor and gift for banter.

SECOND CHANCE AT LOVE

Be Sure to Read These New Releases!

TWO'S COMPANY #412
by Sherryl Woods

WINTER FLAME #413
by Kelly Adams

A SWEET-TALKIN' MAN #414
by Jackie Leigh

TOUCH OF MIDNIGHT #415
by Kerry Price

HART'S DESIRE #416
by Linda Raye

A FAMILY AFFAIR #417
by Cindy Victor

Order on opposite page

SECOND CHANCE AT LOVE

___	0-425-09744-7	A HINT OF SCANDAL #385 Dana Daniels	$2.25
___	0-425-09745-5	CUPID'S VERDICT #386 Jackie Leigh	$2.25
___	0-425-09746-3	CHANGE OF HEART #387 Helen Carter	$2.25
___	0-425-09831-1	PLACES IN THE HEART #388 Delaney Devers	$2.25
___	0-425-09832-X	A DASH OF SPICE #389 Kerry Price	$2.25
___	0-425-09833-8	TENDER LOVING CARE #390 Jeanne Grant	$2.25
___	0-425-09834-6	MOONSHINE AND MADNESS #391 Kate Gilbert	$2.25
___	0-425-09835-4	MADE FOR EACH OTHER #392 Aimee Duvall	$2.25
___	0-425-09836-2	COUNTRY DREAMING #393 Samantha Quinn	$2.25
___	0-425-09943-1	NO HOLDS BARRED #394 Jackie Leigh	$2.25
___	0-425-09944-X	DEVIN'S PROMISE #395 Kelly Adams	$2.25
___	0-425-09945-8	FOR LOVE OF CHRISTY #396 Jasmine Craig	$2.25
___	0-425-09946-6	WHISTLING DIXIE #397 Adrienne Edwards	$2.25
___	0-425-09947-4	BEST INTENTIONS #398 Sherryl Woods	$2.25
___	0-425-09948-2	NIGHT MOVES #399 Jean Kent	$2.25
___	0-425-10048-0	IN NAME ONLY #400 Mary Modean	$2.25
___	0-425-10049-9	RECLAIM THE DREAM #401 Liz Grady	$2.25
___	0-425-10050-2	CAROLINA MOON #402 Joan Darling	$2.25
___	0-425-10051-0	THE WEDDING BELLE #403 Diana Morgan	$2.25
___	0-425-10052-9	COURTING TROUBLE #404 Laine Allen	$2.25
___	0-425-10053-7	EVERYBODY'S HERO #405 Jan Mathews	$2.25
___	0-425-10080-4	CONSPIRACY OF HEARTS #406 Pat Dalton	$2.25
___	0-425-10081-2	HEAT WAVE #407 Lee Williams	$2.25
___	0-425-10082-0	TEMPORARY ANGEL #408 Courtney Ryan	$2.25
___	0-425-10083-9	HERO AT LARGE #409 Steffie Hall	$2.25
___	0-425-10084-7	CHASING RAINBOWS #410 Carole Buck	$2.25
___	0-425-10085-5	PRIMITIVE GLORY #411 Cass McAndrew	$2.25
___	0-425-10225-4	TWO'S COMPANY #412 Sherryl Woods	$2.25
___	0-425-10226-2	WINTER FLAME #413 Kelly Adams	$2.25
___	0-425-10227-0	A SWEET TALKIN' MAN #414 Jackie Leigh	$2.25
___	0-425-10228-9	TOUCH OF MIDNIGHT #415 Kerry Price	$2.25
___	0-425-10229-7	HART'S DESIRE #416 Linda Raye	$2.25
___	0-425-10230-0	A FAMILY AFFAIR #417 Cindy Victor	$2.25
___	0-425-10513-X	CUPID'S CAMPAIGN #418 Kate Gilbert	$2.50
___	0-425-10514-8	GAMBLER'S LADY #419 Cait Logan	$2.50

Available at your local bookstore or return this form to:

SECOND CHANCE AT LOVE
THE BERKLEY PUBLISHING GROUP, Dept. B
390 Murray Hill Parkway, East Rutherford, NJ 07073

Please send me the titles checked above. I enclose _____. Include $1.00 for postage and handling if one book is ordered; add 25¢ per book for two or more not to exceed $1.75. CA, NJ, NY and PA residents please add sales tax. Prices subject to change without notice and may be higher in Canada. Do not send cash.

NAME_____

ADDRESS_____

CITY_____ STATE/ZIP_____

(Allow six weeks for delivery.)

Highly Acclaimed Historical Romances From Berkley

_____ 0-425-10006-5 **Roses of Glory**
$3.95 by Mary Pershall
From the author of <u>A Triumph of Roses</u> comes a new novel about a knight and his lady whose love defied England's destiny.

_____ 0-425-09472-3 **Let No Man Divide**
$4.50 by Elizabeth Kary
An alluring belle and a handsome, wealthy shipbuilder are drawn together amidst the turbulence of the Civil War's western front.

_____ 0-425-09218-6 **The Chains of Fate**
$3.95 by Pamela Belle
Warrior and wife, torn apart by civil war in England, bravely battle the chains of fate that separate them.

_____ 0-515-09082-4 **Belle Marie**
$3.95 by Laura Ashton
A tempestuous saga of a proud Southern family who defied the rules of love—and embraced their heart's wildest desires.

Available at your local bookstore or return this form to:

THE BERKLEY PUBLISHING GROUP
Berkley • Jove • Charter • Ace
THE BERKLEY PUBLISHING GROUP, Dept. B
390 Murray Hill Parkway, East Rutherford, NJ 07073

Please send me the titles checked above. I enclose _____. Include $1.00 for postage and handling if one book is ordered; add 25¢ per book for two or more not to exceed $1.75. CA, NJ, NY and PA residents please add sales tax. Prices subject to change without notice and may be higher in Canada. Do not send cash.

NAME_____

ADDRESS_____

CITY_____ STATE/ZIP_____

(Allow six weeks for delivery.)